Shinglebolt

By
Jean Cummings

Illustrations by Jane Stroschin

Copyright © 2000
Jean Cummings

All rights reserved. No part of this book may be reproduced in any form, except for the inclusion of brief quotations in a review, without permission in writing from the author or publisher.

Rx Ranch Enterprises
2609 E. Fruitport Road
Spring Lake, Michigan 49456

ISBN: 0-9679959-3-0
Second Edition, December, 2000

Other titles by Jean Cummings:
Why They Call Him the Buffalo Doctor
Alias The Buffalo Doctor
Buffalo in Our Backyard
Stardancer

Printed in the USA by
Morris Publishing
3212 East Highway 30
Kearney, NE 68847 • 800-650-7888

Contents

1	Alone in the Big Woods	1
2	Hodag Got Him!	13
3	Shinglebolt is His Name	23
4	Pa Meets Shinglebolt	29
5	The "Mess" Hall	39
6	Four Peach Pies!	49
7	Cork Pine and Pemmican	57
8	Murder in the Big Woods	63
9	Awful News	71
10	The Crack of a Rifle	77
11	Catch the Murdering Thieves!	83
12	Gerry's Rocks Ahead!	91
13	"The Haunt" No Longer	99
14	Snowtown Piers Threatens	105
15	Spirit Dog or Dog of Spirit	113

Illustrations

A "Hodog" saves Corky	21
A real "mess" hall!	41
Shinglebolt helps out	49
Shinglebolt and Three Paws	55
The Rescue	119

All five illustrations as well as the front cover drawing of Corky and Shinglebolt are the work of Jane Stroschin.

Introduction

This book was conceived when my husband and I bought a charming log home on the banks of the Muskegon River between Hardy and Rogers dams. The home was built in the 1930s with logs called "deadheads"—stray logs which sank during the lumbering times of the 19th century.

The builder of the home salvaged these logs from the muddy river bottom and milled the lumber in his own sawmill located on a millstream on the property.

I became fascinated with the Muskegon River and researched its history in the Big Rapids Public Library. When our family moved to Muskegon, located at the mouth of the Muskegon River, the extensive materials of Hackley Public Library were available, and I studied the background of the lower reaches of the river. While reading old newspapers, I saw a news item about a St. Bernard dog found wandering in the woods, apparently having become separated from a traveling sideshow. Years of owning and raising St. Bernards had honed my interest in this giant breed and my imagination ignited.

Originally I had intended to write a history of the Muskegon River. However, I realized that such a book would have limited readership. I decided instead to place a fictional plot within the historical background. It is my hope that in this way more people will read about the glorious days of lumbering on the mighty Muskegon River.

Jean Cummings

Readers' Comments

"Shinglebolt was so fascinating my household chores went undone until I finished reading it."
Ruth Landes, nonagenarian

"Shinglebolt will do very well in Michigan schools.... a boy, big dog, accurate history and a fun story....you've got a winner here!"
Jane Stroschin, illustrator and former children's librarian

"Andrew and I just finished reading Shinglebolt last night. We finished it in a record four nights. Storytime each evening was lengthened from our regular 30 minutes to 90 minutes as neither of us could bear to put the book down. We both enjoyed learning about logging in the Muskegon area and how the loggers lived, and the adventures of Corky and Shinglebolt held Andrew's attention throughout the book."
Monica Carman, mother of pre-schooler.

"Can't wait to see it as a movie!"
Nancy Goodman

"The reader can see the terrain and smell the vegetation. The suspense keeps the readers' attention in a yarn of loyalty, values and acceptance. This book should have great appeal to youth as well as adults."
Larry Madsen

Chapter 1
Alone in the Big Woods

With the toe of his boot Corky Barden nudged a smooth stone out of the mud and gave it a kick into the dark river. Dusk was changing the deep green woods to purple. In another hour everything would be black. Corky shivered, the lump in his throat swelled. He'd never felt so lonely or so frightened.

Brushing his black hair out of his eyes, he looked back down river again, hoping to see what he was waiting for—the sight of Cadje in his birchbark canoe gliding swiftly up the Muskegon River. But there was nothing—only the slow sliding water surrounded by dense forest.

The faint sound of footsteps on stones made Corky jump; he squinted at a clump of willows upstream. Something was moving through those bushes. His fingers tightened around his only weapon, an oak branch. The dim shape moved out of the willows and onto the sandbar, where it stopped at the water's edge. Corky could make out a white snout and bushy black-ringed tail. When he saw the black mask over the creature's eyes, he breathed in relief. It was only a coon coming down to the water to wash its food.

Corky sighed. Yesterday when he ran away, he'd never expected to spend a night alone in the woods. Wolves prowled these Michigan forests. Many times he'd seen settlers bring in wolf hides, to collect their eight-dollar bounty from the sheriff. He might meet a black bear coming down to water, or a lynx could jump on him from an overhead branch. Being stranded all alone out here had not been part of his plan.

Cadjetan Padou was supposed to start up river yesterday afternoon. Corky had expected Cadje to overtake him before he got so far as Mill Iron. But Corky had trudged past the tiny villages at Mill Iron and Maple Island, and later, when he passed under the bridge at Bridgeton, there was still no sign of Cadje. Last night when darkness fell, Corky had built a huge campfire on a sandbar and had huddled near it all night. He hadn't slept much. The nighttime noises of the forest scared him. Cracking, splitting sounds jerked him wide awake. Howls and screeches tightened his clutch on his stout branch.

At dawn he'd plodded onward, his empty stomach growling. How he wished there had been more food in his lunch pail! Yesterday afternoon he'd eaten everything—the apples, bread, and biscuits, so sure he would be joined by Cadje any moment.

Corky felt beat out. Why doesn't Cadje come? he moaned. In disgust, he kicked another rock and flopped down on the river bank, after another glance down river.

Ever since his mother died when he was four years old, Corky had lived with his Aunt Phoebe in the bustling sawmill town of Muskegon on the eastern shore of Lake Michigan. Aunt Phoebe was nice—a round, jolly person. From June to September Pa lived with them, and that made summers wonderful. But Pa was a lumberman. Each fall he left to go up the Muskegon River to the logging camp he owned. He didn't return until his thousands of logs were floated down the river in late spring.

Every autumn Corky begged, "Please, Pa, take me with you."

But always Pa insisted that Corky stay in Muskegon to get his school-learning. "I understand that you want to go with me, Corky, and I want to be with you, too. But you've got to get your ciphering and reading," Pa always said. "If you're going to be my partner someday, I want a smart partner."

This autumn Corky felt crushed when Pa said "no" again. He supposed he could have stood another winter with Aunt Phoebe; but in August things had changed for the worse.

Aunt Tishia arrived from Illinois and moved into their house. Jolly Aunt Phoebe decided to pay a long-overdue visit to her brother in Chicago since Tishia would be with Corky. Aunt Phoebe left on the next schooner sailing for Chicago, promising to return in time for Christmas. Aunt Tishia took over the household.

Corky couldn't understand how two sisters could be so different. Where Aunt Phoebe was stout and cheerful, Aunt Tishia was skinny and cranky. She wouldn't allow him an after-school snack, no matter how hungry he was, and she didn't bake delicious-smelling goodies as Aunt Phoebe had. Meals took on a terrible sameness. Aunt Tishia boiled a big pot of meat and vegetables together and served the stuff for meals until it was all gone. How Corky yearned for Aunt Phoebe's crusty fried cakes or her juicy prune bread!

Aunt Tishia got on Pa's nerves while he was still there. She wouldn't let him smoke his pipe in the house or bring his woodsman friends inside.

"Your friends smell, Julius!" her sharp voice shrilled. "I won't have them stinking up my house."

Pa had to put up with Aunt Tishia for only two weeks. Then it was time for him to go up river where he would supervise getting his lumber camp underway for the logging season which began in October.

The day Pa left, Corky slouched on the front stoop, staring at his father's departing back. Suddenly, Pa had turned and come back to the steps.

"Brace up, son," Pa had patted Corky on the shoulder. "Maybe next year you can go with me for a month or so." Pa hesitated a moment longer, a worried frown on his ruddy, freckled face. Then he was gone.

Corky's spirits brightened. With the half-promise that he might be allowed to go up river with Pa next year, he tried to bear Aunt Tishia. But it was awful. She didn't want him to have any fun.

She forbade him to go down to the docks anymore. "Those are rough, wild people down there," she said. "It's no place for a young gentleman to dawdle. You are never to go there again. It's going to be hard enough for me to squelch that savage blood in you."

Corky scowled. For years he'd spent his happiest hours at the wharves, watching the graceful schooners swallow their cargoes of milled lumber. How he loved hearing the sailors tell their tales of faroff ports and stormy seas!

Corky's dark eyes narrowed, and he stalked away, furious. Call me a savage, will she! Might as well call me a dum injun like Freddie Stone does.

Even good-natured Aunt Phoebe didn't like Corky's having Indian blood. She never mentioned that "shameful" fact. Instead, she often reminded Corky that his father came from an excellent family, and that he should be proud to bear the name "Barden." As for Corky's half-Indian mother, Aunt Phoebe pretended she never had existed.

Corky wished he could remember his mother better. He remembered crying a lot after she died because he'd missed her so much. He couldn't quite picture his mother's face. Pa talked about her sometimes. Pa said she was beautiful, with straight black hair so long she could sit upon it. Her father was a teacher out East, and her mother, Corky's grandmother, a lovely Onondaga woman. Once, Pa told Corky, "Your mother was the smartest woman I ever knew. She could speak five languages. She had a better education than I, and she was a lady. Yet when I brought her here to Muskegon, the women called her "injun," or "squaw," and were rude to her—she the finest lady in town! Can you imagine?"

Corky *could* imagine, but he didn't say so to Pa. Never would he go whining to Pa about the times Freddie Stone spit at him, or when Maribelle Stearn called him a skinny papoose. He'd almost gotten used to being treated with scorn, as somebody inferior, because his mother was Indian. He didn't understand why. It was just the way things were.

Corky didn't feel like an Indian. He didn't know anything about the woods, hunting, birchbark, or trade beads—those things Indians were supposed to know about. He had straight black hair and brown eyes, but many of his German and French schoolmates were darker and more Indian-looking than he.

He shrugged. Aunt Tishia could call him a savage if she wanted, but she couldn't keep him away from the docks. He'd go down there no matter what she said.

So many things stirred Corky's wish to be with Pa. There was that beckoning sound of the migrating wild geese. Fallen leaves floating in the rain barrel signaled that winter was on its way. In spite of these urgings, Corky knew he might be in Muskegon yet, if he hadn't met Cadje while walking to school yesterday morning.

"Bonjour." The Indian's brown face wrinkled into a smile. Deep lines creased the outer corners of his dark eyes. "Any words to your Pa? I start up river after noon."

Corky's eyes lit up. "Are you going to canoe up to camp?"

Cadje nodded. "Oui. I drop supplies off at Haunt's on way. Then I go to camp."

"No news, I guess," Corky shook his head. "Just tell Pa I'm doing all right."

The Indian padded off down the sawdust sidewalk. Thoughtfully, Corky stared after Cadje, a strange figure, his clothes showing exactly what he was—a mixture of his Ottawa Indian ancestry and a French grandfather who came with the American Fur Company to Michigan when it was still a territory, married Cadje's Ottawa grandmother, and settled down to trapping for furs. Like the other lumberjacks, or "shanty boys," as they called themselves, he wore a red-and-black checkered wool mackinaw shirt and gray trousers with a red-and-white knit stocking cap pulled tight over his head. But not forsaking his Indian ancestry, Cadje sported a long eagle feather pierced through his shanty boy's hat, and instead of clumping along in heavy calked boots, his feet moved silently in doeskin moccasins. Cadje was an odd man, yet no one ever ridiculed him. How Corky envied him. If only he could be going to Pa's camp, too.

Cadje disappeared into Slezak's blacksmith shop, and Corky sauntered on to school, where Christopher Columbus became the final push that drove Corky to run away.

Corky ignored the game of Red Rover going on in the schoolyard. He strolled inside to sit at his desk where he could think quietly, envying Cadje his journey to Pa's camp.

Blond, pink-cheeked Miss Swensen, was writing lessons on the big slate board. Her ruffled, green-and-white checked gingham frock swayed gracefully as she wrote. Corky liked his pretty teacher, and especially her sing song Scandinavian accent. He knew that she liked him, too, because he was well-behaved and prepared in his daily lessons.

Miss Swensen stepped to the doorway and rang the brass hand bell. When the assembled students became quiet in their seats, she began.

"This is a special day. Who knows what we're celebrating today?"

Annabelle Sherman's hand shot up. "October 12, 1492."

"That's right, Annabelle," said Miss Swensen. "Will someone else tell me what happened that day?"

Freddie Stone waggled his arm furiously. "Christopher Columbus discovered America!" he shouted. Freddie grinned. He didn't have correct answers very often.

A loud voice sneered, "That's what *you* think!" Corky blinked as he realized that the voice was his own. Dimly, he heard gasps and muffled giggles around him.

Miss Swensen's round face darkened like a ripe plum. "Corky Barden! What did you say?"

Again with surprise, Corky heard his own voice speak. "Freddie Stone is full of beans! It's just like him to think that Christopher Columbus discovered America."

Miss Swensen's blue eyes were ice. "It happens that Freddie Stone is absolutely correct, young man. Now you will apologize to him."

Corky's lower lip pursed stubbornly. "He's not right, so I don't owe him an apology."

The teacher snatched up her wooden ruler and stepped toward Corky. "Just who do *you* think discovered America?" she asked quietly through tight lips.

"My forefathers—the Indians—discovered America long before Columbus was born." Corky raised his chin higher. "My father told me so."

There was silence while the teacher thought this over. Then she advanced toward Corky until she stood directly over his seat. "True, the Indians were here first," she admitted. "However, they didn't report their discovery to the world, so they can't be considered actual discoverers. Christopher Columbus has the rightful honor. Master Barden, you will now apologize to Freddie Stone."

Corky stared openmouthed at Miss Swensen. How could she deny that the Indians discovered America?

"Apologize! Now!" she ordered, raising the ruler.

"Never!" Corky cried, lurching from his desk. The ink bottle tipped out of its hole in his desk and fell onto the plank floor. Nearby girls screamed as flecks of dark ink spattered their frocks. Corky fled through the cloakroom, grabbing his jacket and lunch pail, and raced out into the schoolyard, leaving behind the cries and wails.

He kept running at full speed until he was out of sight of the small schoolhouse. He slowed to a jog, gasping for breath.

"I hate them! I hate them all!" he sputtered. "Oh, Pa, why did you leave me?"

The masts of the lumber schooners in the harbor towered over the roofs of the houses to his left. Corky scurried around a corner, heading northeast, away from the wharves and hateful people. He walked on thoughtfully as the plan began to come to him, spreading out in his mind. Of course! It was the only thing he could do.

Pa trusted Cadjetan Padou more than any other man alive. Corky could get to Pa through Cadje. Corky knew the Indian would never help him run away. But Corky reasoned that if he could get far enough up river before Cadje overtook him in the canoe, surely he would pick Corky up. All Corky had to do was keep walking up river, and sometime in the afternoon Cadje would come paddling along, and Corky could ride with him to Pa's logging camp.

And I'm not really running *away*, Corky told himself. I'm running *to* my father.

The plan had seemed perfect, and it had worked out fine in the beginning.

Corky had skirted around the shanties of Pickett Town at the mouth of the river. There lived mostly trappers, Indians, and some of the booming-ground hands. Corky knew too many of them to risk being seen. For a long time he kept away from the river. The lower end of the river, just before it widened into Muskegon Lake, was the log-booming grounds. There dozens of wooden platforms jutted out over the river. The booming crews stood on these platforms to snag and sort the logs floating downstream. The end of each log was branded with a mark showing who owned that log. The men dancing along these narrow plank walkways looked at each log's brand, and then guided it to its proper destination. Many of the men at the booming company knew Corky. He didn't want to face any questions of "Why aren't you in school?"

The trees grew more dense and the tangled undergrowth made walking slow and difficult. At last Corky reckoned he was beyond the booming-grounds. He turned north, stumbling through brush and ducking low branches. Finally he saw an opening in the forest, which meant the river.

At the water's edge he squatted, splashing his hands in the clear water. It made him feel closer to Pa, knowing that these drops of river water had passed by Pa's camp before reaching here.

So happy was he to be heading toward Pa's logging camp that he broke into a trot. Following the shore was much easier than stumbling through the woods. Sometimes the trees closed in, growing right to the river's edge. On either side of the river the land stretched flat and low. The endless reeds and cattails told him that although the land was dry and above water now, much of the year it must be marshy. This was new country to Corky. Never before had he ventured above the booming grounds.

He tramped on, whistling a cheery tune. Since Cadje was to start out in the afternoon, Corky was certain the faster canoe would catch up with him before nightfall.

But it hadn't. No welcome canoe had appeared. And now a second twilight was approaching.

Whatever had happened to Cadje? Corky groaned, hugging his bony knees to his empty belly. In addition to hunger pains, his head throbbed. His feet hurt from trudging miles of rugged shoreline, sometimes through marshes, tripping over unseen logs half-smothered in mud.

A twilight hush began to settle over the wild forest like a fog. Pine needles stopped their friendly whispering, and the twittering of the birds faded as they chose their roosts and slept. With a sigh Corky heaved himself onto his painful feet. He must gather firewood. The air was chilling, but Corky shivered from fear. Another night alone in the woods seemed more than he could bear. Then he thought of living with Aunt Tishia. He clamped his jaw hard to stop his chattering teeth and began searching for kindling and dry logs.

When a huge fire was crackling, Corky pulled off his boots and socks and limped to the river's edge. Rolling up his pant legs, he waded in, sighing as the cold water numbed the pain of his blistered toes and heels. As he stood there, staring into the near-darkness, a movement down river caught his attention. He squinted, shielding his eyes from the campfire. There! He saw it again!—a flicker of something pale moving in the river.

Corky's heart pounded as he stared. Yes, yes—it was a canoe!

"Hullo, the canoe!" he shouted. "Hullo! Hullo!"

The birchbark canoe skimmed into the firelight. With a crunch, the canoe was beached on the smooth sand. The wiry figure of Cadjetan Padou jumped ashore. The man's brown face scowled. Standing ankle-deep in the river, Corky stared wide-eyed at his rescuer. As Cadje leaped toward him, Corky didn't know if he was going to be hugged or slapped.

The Indian did neither. His face smoothed out. For a moment Corky feared the man was going to cry.

"What you do?" Cadje grunted. With a quick movement he scooped Corky into his arms and carried him to the warm fire.

While a hearty supper bubbled in the cook pot, the Indian gently bathed Corky's feet with a dark, strong-smelling liquid. Then Corky was made to swallow a cup of steaming willow bark tea.

"For pain, and make you sleep," Cadje explained.

Not until after Corky had eaten did Cadje insist upon an explanation. The cozy fire, his full stomach, and the willow bark tea combined to make Corky very sleepy. He tried to explain to Cadje why he would no longer stay in Muskegon.

"I know Pa will understand, Cadje. I know he'll let me stay with him at camp," Corky insisted. "Pa wouldn't.." His voice faded, and he slept.

※　　　　　※　　　　　※

For a long time Cadjetan Padou didn't sleep. Sitting crosslegged, he stared into the glowing logs. The animal sounds from the dark woods he hardly heard, they being so familiar, and he having slept among these noises all his life. But what to do with this runaway boy? What would Julius Barden want him to do? This was strange problem, big worry. Should Cadje return him to that skinny old crow aunt? Or should he take him to his father?

The old aunt had put up a squawking fuss when she discovered the boy had run off. Cadje could still see her raisin eyes snapping with anger when she found him.

"You find Mr. Barden's son and deliver him to me!" she cried. "He's probably sneaking around that horrible wharf somewhere."

For twenty-four hours Cadje had searched everywhere, through Bluffton, Muskegon, Pickett Town. No one had seen Corky Barden. Cadje began to fear that the boy had stowed away on an outbound schooner.

Finally, when Cadje had satisfied himself that Corky was not in Muskegon, he had started up river, dreading the message he must carry to Julius Barden. And now he had found the boy, but what should he do?

Barden would expect Cadje to arrive at the logging camp tonight or tomorrow. Already he was a day behind. If he took the boy to Muskegon, he would lose another day. But Julius Barden had left the boy in Muskegon, so that was where he should be.

Cadje frowned. Barden expected him to do the right thing. For ten years Barden had been his boss. They trusted each other, like partners. Cadje had taught Barden how to survive in the forest. Barden had taught Cadje to read and write and cipher. Barden was more than a boss. He was a friend.

And what to do with this friend's only child? Cadje thought back thirty years ago when he was a boy living in the Indian village at Old Woman's Bend. Winter months, his father was gone much, hunting and trapping. But when Cadje was younger than this boy his father had begun taking him along, teaching him the way of the woods. The father had been killed during Cadje's thirteenth winter, but Cadje had been taught well, and he survived. He had begun a man's work, hunting meat for his mother's cook pot and trapping for furs which they traded. He remembered his mother's happy face when he brought her a tin dish pan. She had hung it around her neck as an ornament until Cadje showed her what it could be used for. Cadje closed his eyes. He almost could smell maple syrup boiling over his mother's fire.

But that was long ago. Cadje shook his head. He pulled off his stocking cap and ruffled his thatch of thick black hair. He didn't know what he should do.

After banking the fire Cadje rolled up in his blanket beside the sleeping boy. *In morning I decide*, he thought.

Chapter 2
Hodag Got Him!

It was already daylight before Corky began to stir. For a moment the odor of frying side pork fooled him into thinking he was back in his own bed with jolly Aunt Phoebe preparing breakfast down in the kitchen. Far above him the green roof of pine needles told him he was out in the big woods. But the cooking aroma reminded him he was no longer alone. Cadje had come along, after all, though a whole day later than Corky had expected. To think that the whole frightening time he'd been waiting for Cadje, Cadje had been searching for him in Muskegon!

Wincing, Corky pulled his boots over his sore feet and limped to the fire. Cadje squatted over an iron skillet, lifting out crisp, curling pieces of browned side pork. Into the sputtering grease he poured thick batter for flapjacks. Corky licked his lips. He'd never been so hungry.

After they had eaten, Corky took the skillet to the river to scour it with sand and gritty snake grass. Cadje began stowing gear in the canoe, rearranging the supplies to make room for Corky in the bow.

"When will we get to The Haunt's place?" Corky asked as he handed Cadje the clean pan.

With a grunt, the Indian pulled a rope taut over the supply bundle, securing it to the canoe. "We not go there," he said without looking at Corky. "I take you to Muskegon where your Pa said you be."

Corky's lips tightened. He thrust his narrow jaw outward. "Go ahead! Take me back! But as soon as you're out of sight, I'll leave again. I'll come back alone!"

A cunning thought came to him. "I'll get to Pa all by myself. That is, if a wolf doesn't get me, or a bear, or I don't get drowned if I build a raft." He peered slyly at Cadje to see what effect this had.

Though the brown face stared sternly at him, Corky frowned back defiantly, hoping Cadje would see how determined he was.

Cadje exploded into a gabble of sounds which made no sense to Corky—a mixture of French, Ottawa, and English. The grumbling finally ended. Cadje motioned Corky to climb into the canoe.

Corky held his breath. Which way would Cadje turn the canoe—upstream to Pa, or downstream to Aunt Tishia?

Cadje's shove pushed the canoe backwards into the stream. This time of year there was little current, and they seemed to stand still. Corky glanced over his shoulder toward the stern. Cadje sat motionless, holding the paddle across his lap. Corky shut his eyes, squeezing them tight, thinking, "Upstream, upstream," trying by the strength of his will to force the canoe to swing upstream. With a drumbeat rhythm he kept repeating to himself. *Upstream, upstream,* until he felt his whole body and even the canoe, join in the beat. Slowly he opened his eyes. The surrounding forest was sliding by—they were moving! He looked back for their campsite, and a joyful gasp caught in his lungs as he discovered they were moving upstream.

"Yahoo!" Corky exploded. He swung around to give Cadje a grateful grin.

"Go up river harder than go down river," the Indian said, sliding the spare paddle toward Corky. "You help."

So happy was he to be going to Pa at last, Corky bent into stroking with furious sweeps of the paddle. The water churned and splashed as he dipped the paddle in and out, in and out. Soon he was panting for breath.

"*Non,* boy," called Cadje. "You wear out. Watch me."

Corky watched carefully. When he returned to paddling, he tried to imitate Cadje's graceful, long strokes.

When the sun reached the center of its arc, where it could shine down directly onto the opening in the forest made by the river, Corky was paddling easily with little effort. His arm muscles were bearing up, but the palms of his hands were blistered.

With relief, he saw Cadje point the canoe toward shore.

"We noon here," Cadje grunted.

They beached the canoe on a V-shaped sandbar formed by a creek entering the river at this point. A short distance up the creek was a beaver dam forming a wide swamp behind it. From the reeds came the rhythmic croaking of frogs.

"I look around," said Cadje, as he headed up the creek.

While Corky moved about, gathering firewood and starting the cook fire, he noticed that no tall pine trees grew here. Instead, a dense thicket of trembling aspen choked out everything but an occasional hemlock or drooping tamarack. Though he felt no breeze, the yellowing aspen leaves constantly quivered and shook. Corky understood why Pa called them "quaking aspen." Pa said his superstitious woodsmen feared the quaking aspen, believing it to be an unlucky tree. Nothing in a lumber camp could be made from its soft wood, the lumberjacks insisted. The smooth, gray aspen bark had a silver glow, and the dancing leaves seemed to whisper. Corky thought the trembling trees were pretty. "Eh, see what I find," called Cadje.

Corky hurried toward Cadje, who was crouched beside a fallen aspen. Trapped beneath the trunk and branches of the fallen tree squirmed a dying beaver, feebly baring his long, curved teeth at them. A blow with a flat rock stopped the beaver's suffering. With a heave, Cadje rolled the trunk off the furry animal.

"We have big feast tonight," he grinned. "Haunt like beaver better than anything, and he cook it like squaw do."

"Will we get to The Haunt's tonight?" Corky asked.

"*Oui.* And we be to your Pa's tomorrow night." A worried frown crossed Cadje's forehead. Corky figured Cadje was wondering what Pa would think.

While Cadje dressed out the beaver carcass, Corky studied the beaver dam. He never tired of looking at them. It seemed almost unbelievable that a few animals could design and build a stout dam which could form so large a pond.

"Beaver smart fellow, *oui*?" said Cadje. "See how thick ends of branches all face downstream?"

Corky looked closer at the dam of quaking aspen saplings. Cadje was right. Every single one of the hundreds of small trees and branches were turned the same way. The spreading, branching ends were all pointed upstream toward the wide pond formed by the dam.

Cadje explained. "That real smart of beaver. Leaves and sticks float downstream. Catch in dam better that way. Make dam solid. Mud and weeds fill it tight."

"Why was this beaver cutting down another tree?" Corky asked. "Does the dam need fixing or something?"

"In winter beaver live on bark from aspen tree. Before leaves fall, beaver cut many trees. Store underwater. Cold water keep bark juicy all winter. Beaver stay fat and happy."

When lunch was finished Corky hopped back into the bow of the canoe, eager to be heading on. When he lifted the paddle, a shock of pain crossed his face.

Cadje saw it. "Show hands," he ordered, demonstrating by holding his own brown hands palm upward.

Embarrassed over showing his soft, town-living hands, Corky hung his head when he thrust out his blistered palms.

Again, out came the brown, foul-smelling liquid which Cadje had put on Corky's sore feet the night before. All the time muttering to himself, the Indian rummaged through the large bandana haversack containing his personal belongings and pulled out a pair of deerskin gloves.

"These help," he said, motioning Corky to put them on.

Corky pulled on the gloves, wishing the sting from the brown medicine would let up. As they pushed off from the river bank, a flash of white moving through the dense aspen thicket caught Corky's eye. He looked hard, but it was gone.

A quarter of an hour later he saw again a large white shape moving through the trees. It seemed to be staying even with the canoe.

Corky looked back to see if Cadje had seen it.

"There's something big and white in the woods over there," said Corky, jerking his head toward the left bank.

"Maybe white tail of deer."

"No." Corky shook his head. "It's bigger than that. It's as big, well, as big as a bear!"

Cadje chuckled. "No white bear here. Just black bear."

During the next hour of paddling Corky saw no more movement of white in the timber. Still, he had the uneasy feeling that something was following the canoe—perhaps stalking them.

About mid-afternoon they rounded a sharp bend in the river and came upon a deserted Indian village.

"That my village," said Cadje. "People gone now. In Moon of Turning Leaves they go dig roots and get berries."

As the canoe slid past, Corky gazed at the dozens of round, bark-covered wigwams. It was hard to imagine Cadje living in one of those huts. This must be Old Woman's Bend, he thought. Corky remembered Pa mentioning a large Indian village there.

The afternoon was nearly gone when Corky saw the white thing again. "Look, Cadje!" he cried, pointing. But the white shape was gone in an instant.

"Didn't you see it that time?" he asked, looking hopefully back at Cadje.

The Indian's blank look showed that he had not.

"It's following us, and it's huge!" Corky's dark eyes widened with excitement. "It's bigger than a bear—bigger than a deer! And it's white as falling snow."

Cadje's face crinkled. "Must be Hodag," he said, grinning.

"What's a Hodag?"

"I never see one. Indian don't believe in Hodag," he shrugged. "But shanty boys do. They afraid of Hodag. Some say it have horns. Some say it have forked tail. All say it have red eyes which turn milk sour and curdle cream."

"You mean a Hodag isn't real?" Corky asked.

"It real to shanty boys working in woods. They see big tracks in snow, they get back to camp fast. But I say not real. Hodag only up here," Cadje said, tapping his forehead.

Then what was it that he kept seeing? Corky wondered. The white thing sneaking through the timber was real. And he believed it was following their canoe. For miles it had moved along with them.

"Around next bend we be at Haunt's place," Cadje announced.

Corky wondered what The Haunt would be like. For some reason Pa was always sending supplies to him. He tried to remember what Pa had told him about this strange old man who lived alone, far from other human beings. He recalled Pa saying that The Haunt once had been a professor in the East, but something had driven him to this forest wilderness where he lived apart from people. Pa always had spoken respectfully of him, and shown concern over his welfare. The Haunt was too proud to accept help as a gift, so he traded his handiwork for the supplies Pa sent. Corky had seen some of the fine things made by the old hermit. Carefully fashioned from the softest doeskin were moccasins, fringed shirts, leggings, and pouches decorated with porcupine quills dyed bright colors. Pa said The Haunt did finer work than even the Indian women. As they rounded the bend, Cadje steered the canoe toward the north shore of the river where a steep bank rose sharply fifteen feet above the water. The towering pine trees grew to the very edge of the embankment. After beaching the canoe, Cadje threw a holding line around a stout post which seemed to have been driven into the bank for that purpose.

"Allo, the cabin!" the Indian called.

"I saw you coming," a reedy voice answered.

Corky jumped, startled, as the reply came from directly above them. He looked up at what seemed to be an old, old man, though much of the face was concealed by tangled gray whiskers and moustache. So this was The Haunt! He was dressed entirely in deerskins, though no fringe or colorful quills decorated them.

The old fellow tossed down a braided rope ladder.

"Won't you come up?" he invited them.

"First, unload," said Cadje.

Cadje climbed half-way up the ladder. Corky lifted the supplies from the canoe, heaved them up to Cadje, who passed them on up to The Haunt. There were several sacks of flour, sugar and cornmeal, tins of molasses, bags of dried beans, raisins, and prunes, chunks of side pork, and even coffee and tea. *Pa certainly saw to it that The Haunt ate well*, thought Corky.

"Don't forget beaver," the Indian reminded Corky. Corky heaved the fat carcass up to Cadje.

The Haunt wheezed happily when he saw his gift. "Ah," he rubbed his long, thin fingers together. "Woodland's finest delicacy! We shall feast tonight."

Shucks, thought Corky. *He's happier about that old dead beaver than all the supplies Pa sent.*

After they had climbed to the top of the embankment The Haunt pulled up the ladder, carefully rolling it and tucking it under an arm. Then he turned to study Corky.

Why, the old fellow isn't any taller than I am! Corky realized.

The Haunt asked Cadje, "My friend, who is this?"

"This Julius Barden's son. Called Corky."

Behind the bushy, gray eyebrows the old fellow's pale eyes glittered. He stared hard at Corky for a long time, studying his coarse black hair and dark eyes.

Though Corky cleared his throat and shuffled his feet uneasily, he made himself look straight into those piercing eyes, not wishing to let the crazy old man stare him down.

Finally The Haunt broke into a broad smile. "Well, this is a great pleasure," he said. "I am delighted to meet you, Master Barden, and happy to entertain you as my guest."

Corky stammered, "I .. I'm pleased to meet you, ..sir." He swallowed, feeling uncomfortable. Such fine manners seemed strange coming from a dirty old hermit.

The Haunt's cabin was every bit as strange as its owner. The shack was pieced together from odds and ends of boards, old doors, and bits of driftwood. Corky noticed a bedroll and rock-lined cooking pit in the small clearing. Apparently The Haunt cooked and slept outdoors, at least this time of year. Most people would have built their shanty on the bank of the river, but The Haunt had constructed his shelter back in the woods, the thick growth of timber concealing it from river travelers.

It was dark before the beaver was roasted to The Haunt's satisfaction. As they seated themselves cross-legged around the red embers of the cook fire, Corky looked suspiciously at the peculiar meal served on his tin plate.

Cadje waved a finger at Corky's plate. "Dark meat beaver body. White shivering meat beaver tail. Greens he call 'wild spinach.' Says they keep teeth from falling out."

The one thing on his plate Corky recognized was cornbread. This he tried first, finding it just as good as Aunt Phoebe's. The dark meat of the beaver tasted like wild turkey—delicious; but the white jelly-like meat of the tail was too oily. The greens tasted like medicine. Bad enough to make your teeth fall *out*, Corky thought.

They ate in silence. When their plates were set aside, The Haunt pulled a fat, S-curved pipe from an inner pocket. As he tamped tobacco into the round pipe bowl, he spoke to Corky.

"Are you joining your father?" he asked.

"Yes, sir."

"Ah," he sighed, "that will be a great comfort for Julius. It has been lonely for him since he lost your mother." A strange glitter came into the pale eyes. "Now you can try to keep your father from Snowtown Piers."

"Snowtown Piers?" Corky was puzzled. "What's that?"

"You haven't heard of the spell upon Snowtown Piers?" the thin voice gasped.

The Haunt jumped to his feet and began pacing around the cooking pit. With every stride he pounded one bony fist into the other palm as he continued. "Every year when the logging drives pass through, the ghostly tollgate keeper at Snowtown Piers claims a victim. Some poor soul must drown every spring to satisfy that evil spirit."

"Every year a logger gets killed there?" Corky asked.

The old man's eyes glinted wildly beneath his bristly brows. "Without fail, my boy. Every year. That's the toll charged by Snowtown Piers. Don't let your father pay that toll."

The Haunt seated himself beside Corky. In a lower voice, he continued. "From her deathbed your own mother gave warning. 'Tell Julius to beware of Snowtown Piers,' she said. Those were her final words."

A cold ripple shivered up Corky's spine. He'd never heard about this. Why would his mother say such a thing? And how did this old hermit know about it?

"Where's Snowtown Piers?" he asked.

"Upstream from Muskegon Forks, at a tight bending of the river—an evil, abominable place—created by Satan himself. Persuade your father to give it wide berth. He has been warned by a dying voice. Those who are crossing the bridge to the Great Beyond always tell the truth."

Cadje cleared his throat. "Big pile shinglebolts you got over there." He nodded toward a huge stack of eighteen-inch logs at the edge of the clearing.

The Haunt threw Cadje a cool glance.

"No need to scare boy. You sell them?" Cadje persisted.

"Julius is installing a portable shingle mill this winter. I thought I might cut a few on speculation," the old man replied. "In the meantime I use them for firewood."

Because The Haunt seemed to like talking about spooky things, Corky decided to ask his opinion about the Hodag.

"Sir, have you ever seen a Hodag?"

The snarled, gray beard leaped up and down violently. Alarmed, Corky sucked in his breath, as the old man wheezed and swayed. At last he realized the man was laughing.

"No," replied The Haunt, "I have never seen a Hodag, and never will. Neither will I see a Whirling Wumpus, nor an Agropelter." The whiskers shook violently as he continued chuckling.

"What are they?" Corky wanted to know.

"A Whirling Wumpus is a creature who whirls violently in the tote roads and crushes unsuspecting woodsmen. The Agropelter lives in hollow tree trunks. He throws heavy branches down upon the shanty boys. But don't you believe any of it, son. Shanty boys like to put the blame on mythical creatures, when it's often their own carelessness that does them in."

Corky was puzzled. If there were no such animal as the Hodag, what did he see today following the canoe? And if The Haunt didn't believe in those strangely-named creatures, why did he believe in an evil ghost at Snowtown Piers? Corky frowned. He was roused from his thoughts by The Haunt's voice addressing him.

"Young man, would you please bring one of those shinglebolts over here for the fire?"

"Yes sir." Corky rose and trotted toward the monstrous woodpile at the edge of the thick timber. The cook fire had burned low, and he barely could see where he was going. Dimly, he made out the tall pile of shinglebolts looming ahead of him, but he never reached it.

A screeching, splitting sound hit Corky's ears just as a huge blur of white flew at him. The thing slammed into him with such force that Corky was flung through the air before being dashed into the earth, where he rolled over and over through dry pine needles. As the white thing whirled on the ground with him, there was a thundering crash. The ground beneath his shoulders trembled.

Corky lay sprawled on his back, dizzy from the violent jolt. Grunting and pushing at the crushing weight on top of him, he jerked his head to one side, trying to escape the smothering fur which covered his nose and mouth.

Through the struggle, Corky heard pounding feet and the voice of Cadje bellowing, "Hodag! Hodag got him!"

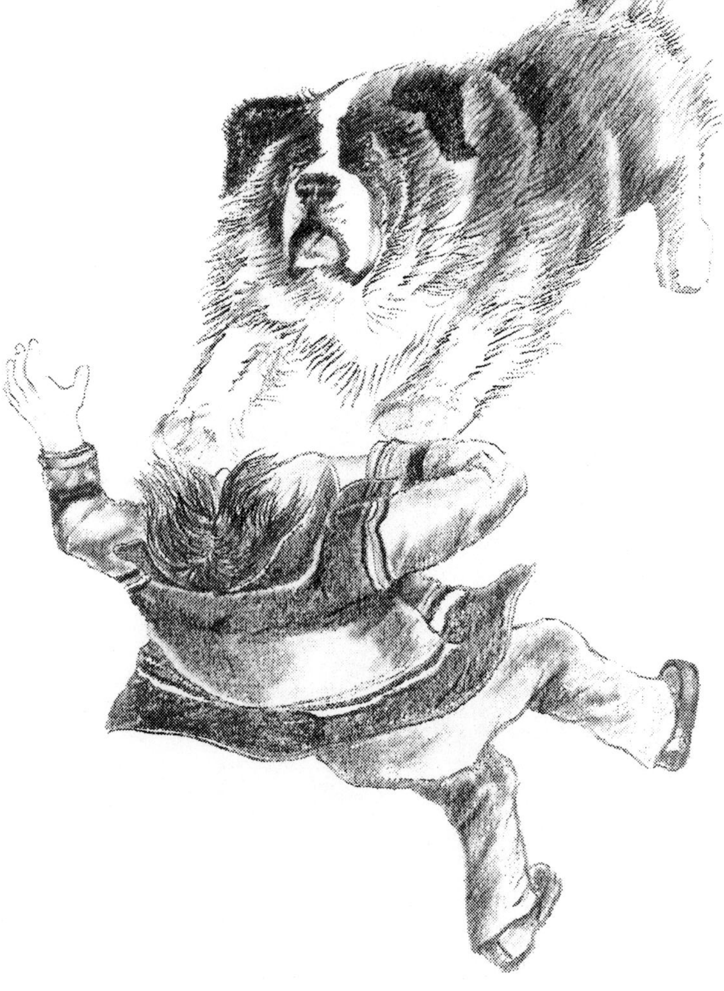

Chapter 3
Shinglebolt is His Name

Corky squeezed his eyes shut against the slimy wet thing sliding over his face. Frantically, he struggled and pushed against the horrible thing.

Cadje's screams drew close. "I get him! I get him!" he yelled.

"No, you fool!" squeaked The Haunt's voice.

Corky heard a dull thud followed by a groan which trailed off into silence.

At last the heavy weight moved off Corky's chest, and he gulped great breaths of air. Rolling over onto his hands and knees, he rubbed his eyes and spit pine needles from his mouth. When he got his eyes open he saw Cadje, sprawled out flat, only an arm's length away. Cadje's right hand clutched a knife.

Gasping, Corky's heart thumped against his ribs. He started to rise, when he noticed The Haunt. The old man knelt a few feet away, patting and stroking a huge, white-and-brown animal.

Still scratching and petting the beast, the old man asked, "Are you all right, son?"

Bewildered, Corky nodded. "But ..but, Cadje?"

"Most unfortunate," said The Haunt. "He will be quite all right, but I had to stop him. He was about to stab your savior here."

Corky squinted through the darkness at the creature being fondled by the spooky hermit.

"Is it ..is it a Hodag?" Corky whispered.

Sputtering, The Haunt cackled, "This heroic soul is no Hodag, boy. But you can call him a Ho-*dog*, if you wish."

Corky stared, mouth open, not understanding.

"This is a *dog*, son!" the old man cried. "Surely you know what a dog is!"

Corky didn't believe that for a minute. The animal was bigger than a full-grown man. Dogs didn't get that big. Corky shivered. Maybe it was some sort of ghost or evil spirit the old hermit had conjured up.

Trembling with fear, Corky dragged his eyes from the strange animal and the old man to poor Cadje, still motionless. On the ground beside the Indian lay a stout shinglebolt. The Haunt must have struck Cadje with that.

Just beyond Cadje lay a monstrous dead branch, a foot in diameter and nearly twenty feet long. *What was that doing there?* Corky wondered.

The Haunt seemed to read his thoughts. "That dead branch nearly crushed you," he explained. "The lumbermen call those falling branches 'widow-makers.' You were saved by your furry canine friend here. With a mighty leap he shoved you out of the way." A shrill giggle came from the bushy beard. "Instead of calling him a Hodag, you should be shaking his paw and thanking him for your safe deliverance."

Not on your life! thought Corky.

With relief, he saw Cadje begin to stir. Grunting, Cadje heaved himself to a sitting position and began rubbing the back of his head. His glazed eyes didn't seem to focus.

Corky crawled to him, touching his sleeve. "Are you all right, Cadje?" he asked.

Suddenly Cadje's eyes focused upon Corky. "Hodag!" he whooped. "Where Hodag?" He tried to rise, but fell back, groaning.

Quietly and firmly The Haunt spoke. "There was no Hodag, Mr. Padou. It was a large dog which managed to save Master Barden here." With a gnarled hand the old man stroked the animal's huge head. "As you can see, he is completely gentle. This particular breed of dog was developed for rescuing humans."

Shaking his head, the Indian squinted suspiciously at the enormous animal. "Dogs not get that big," he said, tightening his grip on the knife.

"Come," said The Haunt. "Let us go over to the fire, where we can see better. I want to bathe your injured head."

Cadje struggled to his feet unsteadily. "Widowmaker clobber me," he muttered, touching the lump rising out of the black hair.

The Haunt threw Corky a warning look, which Corky understood meant, *Let him think the dead branch hit him—for now, anyway.*

Leaning upon each other, Corky and Cadje limped stiffly to the cooking fire, now only embers.

Still holding the strange animal by the scruff of his neck, The Haunt urged it to follow him back to the fire.

"Sit," the old man commanded, thrusting the palm of his hand nearly in the creature's face. Obediently, the spotted animal sat back on its haunches.

"Lie down." It lay down, cradling its huge head between its front paws.

"That's a well-trained dog," The Haunt murmured.

Corky watched the old man bathe the bump on Cadje's head and apply a poultice of wet oak leaves. The Haunt wrapped a red bandana about the Indian's head to hold the poultice against the injured spot.

Corky kept glancing uneasily toward the strange brown-and-white animal. Two fresh logs added to the fire crackled and popped, lighting the clearing brightly. Corky noticed that every time he looked at the animal, its huge, bushy white tail wagged in answer to his glance. It seemed to be a friendly gesture. Though he'd never had a dog of his own, Corky had known many dogs roaming homeless about the docks in Muskegon. With those dogs, their wagging tails meant, "Let's be friends."

Corky studied the animal. Maybe The Haunt *was* right. Perhaps it *was* a dog—a *giant* dog. Even if it hadn't been so big, it was still a funny looking thing. The furry skin on its face hung in folds, and the long ears dangled beside the cheek folds, and such loose skin! As the heat from the fire reached the beast, the big head rose, and its mouth opened, hanging slack. The long, pink tongue slid out, and the animal began to pant and drool. The drooping eyes, slanted downward at their outer corners, gazed gently at Corky.

Hesitantly, Corky edged toward it. The big brown-and-white head cocked to one side eagerly, and the long tail rotated faster.

"Stay back!" warned Cadje from across the fire pit. "That no dog! You ever see dog like that?" he demanded, staring hard at The Haunt.

"No, never before have I seen a living one," admitted The Haunt, "but I've seen pictures of them. I didn't know there were any of the breed in this country."

Finished with tending the Indian's head, the old man seated himself cross-legged beside the fire. "This colossal dog is of a breed raised in Switzerland," he said. "High in the Swiss Alps there is a barren canyon which forms a pass through the snowy peaks. It is called Great St. Bernard Pass. For centuries a group of monks have tended a hospice there to aid travelers crossing the treacherous pass. For three hundred years the monks have raised this powerful breed of dog to locate snowbound and exhausted travelers." The Haunt paused, tapping his pipe bowl against a rock.

"This type of dog is called a St. Bernard," he continued. "An extremely hardy, strong dog, they are famous for their ability to scent people buried in avalanches. Their huge paws enable them to dig victims out of deep snow. They have an excellent sense of direction for leading those rescued to safety at the monastery. If the victim cannot walk, the St. Bernard's loud deep bark carries a great distance to summon help. Only a very large, strong, and intelligent dog could perform such rescues."

Cadje scowled, not convinced. "How you know all that?" he demanded.

The shriveled old man wheezed a deep sigh. "My friend, I have not always dwelt in this wilderness of timber." He spoke softly. "I was once surrounded by books as plentiful as the trees now surrounding me in this vast forest. Those books contained the knowledge of the whole world for any soul who chose to read them. I chose to read a great many. That's where I learned about the background of our gigantic guest here."

Corky stared with new respect at the old man. Pa had said that The Haunt was once a professor. He did seem very smart.

The Haunt stroked his bristly gray moustache thoughtfully. "I can't imagine how a St. Bernard came to be in this territory. Perhaps he became lost from a traveling theatrical company. One can see that he's been living in the woods for some time. Look at his matted coat so tangled with briars. He seems to have become accustomed to the woods and its dangers. His hearing and sense of smell are most acute. They've been sharpened by his efforts to survive."

The Haunt smiled at Corky, creases forming beside his pale eyes. "Don't you like dogs, young man?" he asked. "Our furry friend obviously adores you. See the longing look he casts toward you? He wants you to thank him and make a fuss over him."

Corky's last bit of uneasy fear began to dissolve. Rising, he approached the huge animal. Out of the corner of his eye he saw Cadje stiffen.

The closer Corky stepped, the more violently wagged the bushy tail. As Corky sank to his knees beside the dog, the animal wriggled with joy and began covering Corky's face with wet licks from his long tongue.

So that was the slimy thing he'd felt on his face when the dog was on top of him! When Corky put his arms about the big dog's neck, the dog placed a protective paw on Corky's knee.

The Haunt gave Cadje a piercing look. "Aren't you glad you didn't kill the beast?" The Haunt chewed thoughtfully on his pipe stem. "It will be lonely for the boy at a busy lumber camp, and there are many dangers. Much of the time Julius won't be able to be with the boy. This loyal canine will make an ideal companion for him— a playful chum and a watchful guardian. The dog was sent to this remote wilderness for this purpose."

Cadje leaned closer to The Haunt. "*Who* send dog?" he asked.

Several moments passed before The Haunt answered. "A Power greater than you or I could understand."

Cadje's response was only a whisper. "Great Spirit?"

"That is one of the many names by which It is known."

Corky sat up straight, stopping his playful tussle with the big dog. "I don't know his name!" he cried.

The Haunt chuckled. "His name is 'Shinglebolt.'" The old man's gray eyes twinkled merrily in the waving firelight.

Corky grinned. This was The Haunt's way of saying a shinglebolt had saved the dog from being killed by Cadje's knife.

The old man continued. "The dog obviously was spawned from that pile of shinglebolts over there." He turned to face the Indian. "My friend, you saw him leap from that stack of shinglebolts for his heroic rescue, did you not?"

Cadje grunted and shrugged.

"Hello, Shinglebolt," Corky addressed the big dog, looking deep into the drooping eyes. The tail thumped wildly, and the long tongue washed Corky's cheek.

"There's another name you might prefer," said The Haunt. "About fifty years ago there lived a most famous St. Bernard dog named Old Barry. He rescued a total of forty persons from the treacherous Swiss mountain pass. It is said that he rescued a small boy by getting the boy to climb onto his back, and in that manner carried him to safety. After Old Barry died, his body was preserved and mounted for display. When I was a young man studying in Europe I saw Old Barry at the museum in Berne. To this day, the monks at the hospice name their best dog 'Barry.'"

The old man picked up an ember to relight his pipe. "Perhaps you might wish to name him 'Old Barry?'"

Corky studied the great dog's wrinkled, comical face. Shaking his head, he said, "I like 'Shinglebolt' better." He stroked the downy white fur between the dog's eyes. "How about it, Shinglebolt?"

The St Bernard's bushy white tail rotated violently.

"Shinglebolt! Shinglebolt!" Corky repeated, laughing. "He likes the name 'Shinglebolt!'" Corky threw his arms around the dog's wide shoulders.

"Big dog not hatch from shinglebolts," Cadje protested to The Haunt. "All day boy say he see white animal in woods. I not see—not believe. Now I believe. Big dog follow us all day."

"That may be so," agreed the old man. "But mystery remains. What is this rare dog doing in this remote wilderness, and why did he choose to follow your canoe?" He looked hard at the Indian.

Cadje's troubled face was thoughtful. When he decided, the answer came out softly. "Great Spirit send big dog."

Soberly, the two men stared at each other.

It was very quiet for a long time until Cadje said, "Look. Boy and spirit dog sleep."

Curled against the dog's long body, Corky slept, using a furry shoulder for his pillow. Though the great dog also seemed to be sleeping, he opened his eyes as The Haunt gently laid a deerskin over the boy. Shinglebolt continued to watch protectively until both men rolled up in their robes to sleep.

All through the night the giant dog lay still. Each time a snap echoed through the forest, or a burning fire log crackled, the guarding dog's eyes flew open, not closing again until he was satisfied there was no danger present.

Chapter 4
Pa Meets Shinglebolt

At dawn Corky and Cadje climbed down the rope ladder to the canoe. Corky couldn't tell whether the sun had risen. In these forests the only time he could see the sun was at mid-day when it slid through the shaft of open sky above the river.

When he reached the bottom of the ladder, Corky looked upward into the face of The Haunt, who seemed to be smiling, though it was hard to tell through the tangled beard. Beside The Haunt stood the big St. Bernard, eyes alert, though he was still chewing the remains of the beaver carcass given him for breakfast.

"Cadje!" cried Corky, "how can Shinglebolt get down to the canoe?"

"Spirit dog not go in canoe," the Indian said. "He move wrong, and zap! —over go canoe!"

When Cadje saw Corky's mouth quiver, he reached over quickly and patted his shoulder. "Don' worry," he said. "Dog come. He not leave you. He happy follow on land."

"Do you really think he'll follow us?"

Cadje smiled. "He follow all day yesterday, oui? He hide then. He not afraid anymore. He your friend."

They shoved the canoe away from shore. As they raised their arms in farewell, The Haunt called to Corky. "Young man, tell your father I wish to see you again from time to time."

"Yes sir," Corky called back, wondering why the eerie old fellow would care about seeing him again.

As they paddled upstream, Corky fastened his eyes on the river bank where Shinglebolt sat. When the dog realized the canoe was moving away from him, he heaved himself up and began trotting along the bank after the canoe.

The dog followed, nearly always in sight, as they moved along. Only when he had to get around impassable undergrowth did he disappear for a few moments. After an hour's travel with the dog trailing along, Corky felt more confident that Shinglebolt really would stick with them. The current grew steadily stronger, slowing their forward motion so much that the St. Bernard was able to keep up with them at a slow walk.

Corky began puffing from the exertion of paddling against the increasing current.

"Dam up ahead," Cadje called to him, explaining the swift current. "After portage, river slow again."

When they came to the dam, Corky saw that it was part of a sawmill operation. Several large wooden buildings made up the mill. Huge stacks of sawn lumber lined the river bank between two towering hills of sawdust.

As they beached the canoe, Shinglebolt came running to greet Corky. His black, wet nose nudged Corky affectionately.

"Take rest," Cadje directed. "I talk here, then we go."

Under a small white pine tree Corky and the dog nestled in the mattress of fallen needles. Corky stroked the soft white fur running down the top of Shinglebolt's head until it disappeared into feathery orange fur that formed a cape over the dog's shoulders and back.

"I love you," Corky whispered into a floppy ear.

Shinglebolt's long pink tongue swept across Corky's cheek in response.

Soon two men came out of the largest wooden building and helped Cadje carry the canoe and its contents around the dam. Upstream from the dam the river spread out into a wide backwater impoundment. On the sawmill side of the river hundreds of logs floated, motionless in the still water. Corky understood enough about lumbering to know that these logs would soon be moved into the mill where screeching saws would slice them into smooth boards.

Above the dam there was little current and their canoe cut through the water swiftly. On the left bank Shinglebolt kept alongside, though sometimes he had to break into a lumbering trot to keep up. The river banks grew steeper and higher. On the south bank loomed barren cliffs towering nearly one hundred fifty feet above them. Not a bush nor a vine grew on the scarred slopes.

"That High Rollway," Cadje explained, nodding to the eroded cliff on their right. "All winter shanty boys stack logs at top. Come spring, river deep and fast, they push logs down—whoosh!—into water!"

Corky was so busy checking on Shinglebolt's progress that he didn't look ahead often. Morning was nearly gone when he glanced ahead and was surprised to see the channel apparently coming to a dead end. The river seemed to disappear into a wall of green pine trees.

As they swept closer, Corky saw that the river did not come to an end. Instead, it twisted into a tight bend, looping itself backwards in the direction from which they had come. The river had gouged a big letter "U" for its channel.

Suddenly, a long, shrill howl wailed from out of the woods. The hairs on Corky's neck prickled. The howl rose higher and higher before fading away.

Alarmed, thinking it was a wolf howling, Corky looked around wildly for Shinglebolt. He gasped when he caught sight of the big dog. Almost at the water's edge the St. Bernard sat on his haunches, his massive muzzle tipped toward the sky. Another piercing wail echoed across the river. It was Shinglebolt who was howling!

Corky looked back at Cadje. "What's he doing that for, Cadje? What's the matter with him?"

"He just make noise. Go paddle. He come." His voice stern, the Indian pursed his lips tightly.

Cadje was right. As they paddled through the long, tight bend of the river, they could hear the dog crashing through the trees, following. Every few minutes. though, he stopped to howl his mournful wail.

Two miles farther on Cadje pointed the canoe for shore where they could eat their noon meal. Shinglebolt stood waiting for the canoe to beach, his whole hind end wiggling happily. The dog seemed perfectly normal now. *What could have made him carry on like that back at the bend of the river?*

After they finished eating, Corky asked Cadje about it. "Why do you think Shinglebolt kept howling back there?"

Cadje kept on packing away their tin plates and frying pan. Only a scowl showed that he'd heard Corky's question. Just as Corky had resigned himself to not getting an answer, he spoke.

Without looking up and very quietly, Cadje said, "Where spirit dog howl—that Snowtown Piers."

Corky jumped to his feet and stared down the river, but the U-shaped bend was out of sight, far behind them now. Shinglebolt had howled all the time they were passing Snowtown Piers. But why? Did it have something to do with that spooky legend The Haunt told last night, about Snowtown Piers claiming a victim every year? And The Haunt's warning that he should keep Pa away from there? But how could a dog know anything about that?

The Indian motioned Corky to get into the canoe. Corky tugged at Cadje's sleeve until the Indian finally looked at him.

"Cadje, do you think Shinglebolt howled because he didn't like Snowtown Piers?"

The Indian shrugged. "Don' know." But as they climbed into the canoe he added softly, almost to himself, "Animal sometime know things we not know..."

All afternoon Corky paddled and wondered. Shinglebolt bounded happily along the river's edge. Occasionally he stopped to lap cool water from the river, but never again did he howl or even bark. Corky decided he would ask Pa about it, but he didn't have much hope for an answer. Pa didn't believe in omens or magic. He laughed at the superstitions of his shanty boys, although he had to humor them in their beliefs. No, Corky thought, Pa wouldn't take it seriously. He would just slap his knees, laugh, and say that Shinglebolt had probably smelled a skunk and was complaining about it.

What would Pa think of Shinglebolt, anyway? Corky wondered. He'd been thinking so much about The Haunt and Snowtown Piers that he hadn't considered Pa's reaction to the giant dog. This gave him something more to think about as he dipped the paddle in and out, in and out.

Later, the mighty Muskegon River curled itself into another great loop, bending back upon itself much as it had miles downstream at Snowtown Piers.

"This looks like Snowtown Piers," Corky said,

"Shanty boys call this 'Gerry's Rocks,'" Cadje said. "Jack Monroe, he killed here. They sing song about it much."

River bends were danger points for lumberjacks. Pa had told him how during the big spring log drives, the logs piled up on the tight river bends, causing tremendous jams. Logs kept coming down river and piling up thicker. To break the jams, the daredevil river hogs in their calked boots had to climb over the jammed logs, poking with their peaveys, trying to loosen the key logs and open up the jam. When the certain key log was moved, the jam broke loose, or "hauled," and tons of churning logs flipped through the air like blades of straw. Many a luckless river driver, like the famous Jack Monroe, failed to reach shore safely when the jam hauled. Then they disappeared beneath the thundering avalanche of logs.

Dusk was falling when, with a worried look, Corky turned toward Cadje. "You think Pa will let me keep Shinglebolt, don't you?"

The Indian shrugged. "Find out soon. Camp up ahead," he nodded upstream.

"Which side of the river?" Corky wanted to know.

Cadje jerked his head toward the right bank.

"But Shinglebolt's on the other side of the river!" Corky cried. "How can he get across? Can't we take him in the canoe now?" he pleaded.

"Dogs good swimmers," grunted Cadje.

Ahead, Corky could make out a dock made of logs jutting into the river. Two men stood there, waving, and as they drew closer, Corky recognized one of the figures, his father. As usual, Pa was wearing his lucky wool cap, a strange concoction of red-and-white stripes with a bright green crown.

Once when Corky had asked about the cap's odd colors, Pa had explained. "Your mother knitted me this cap when we were first married. She ran out of red and white yarn, and we didn't have money to buy more, so she finished it with scraps of green yarn."

It made a funny-looking hat, but he had always called it his lucky cap, and it had the advantage of making Pa stand out in a group of woodsmen. Many times in Muskegon Corky had spotted Pa down on the docks because of the green crown and tassel, standing out like a beacon.

Corky laid down his paddle and began waving at Pa with both hands. Pa stopped waving and scratched his head, puzzled.

As Cadje eased the canoe silently against the dock without even a bump, Corky leaped out of the canoe straight into Pa's powerful arms. Held tight in a bear hug, Corky gasped happily, relishing the scratchy feel of Pa's checkered wool shirt against his cheek. The shirt reeked of pipe tobacco, and Corky gulped a silly giggle as he thought how mad Aunt Tishia would be if she sniffed Pa now.

Pa thrust Corky out at arm's length to look at him, and when Corky saw the growth of reddish beard on his father's usually clean-shaven face, he knew he was truly in another way of life now.

"What the tarnation are you doing here?" Pa cried.

Corky could tell by his twinkling eyes that Pa wasn't mad. In fact, he thought Pa seemed real glad to see him.

A worried look suddenly crossed his father's face. "Is something the matter with your Aunt Tishia?"

"Naw, she's fine," Corky answered, trying to look innocent.

Pa turned to Cadje. "How come, Cadje?"

The Indian went right on lifting bundles out of the canoe. Without looking at his boss, he mumbled, "Long story."

Just then Corky remembered the big dog. He searched the bank across the river, but in the purple dusk he could see nothing. "Cadje, where's Shinglebolt?" he cried.

Cadje pointed to the ripples of a wake just on the other side of the docked canoe. The big head was gliding smoothly through the water. When the dog's paws touched bottom, Shinglebolt scrambled quickly ashore.

A collective "Ohhh!" rumbled from the group of shanty boys gathered on the river bank. The men moved backward several steps.

Dripping, Shinglebolt stood motionless for a moment, surveying all the strangers, then gave a tremendous shake to dry himself. As water sprayed in all directions, the shanty boys leaped away, stumbling and bumping each other in confusion.

"Shinglebolt!" Corky yelled. "I'm so glad to see you!" Running down the dock to the wet dog, he knelt and threw his arms around the dripping, broad chest. Shinglebolt's tail churned as he placed a muddy paw on Corky's shoulder.

Pa was sputtering good and loud. "What kind of beast is that?" he bellowed. "Cadjetan Padou! You stop unloading and start talking. I want some answers!"

Cadje straightened up. Jerking his head toward Shinglebolt, he said, "That spirit dog."

"Spirit dog, my peavey!" Pa snorted. "That's a St. Bernard! Where'd you get him?"

"He get *us*," answered Cadje. "He track us, follow us. See him first near Steamboat Landing."

Pa scratched his bristly red whiskers. "What's a St. Bernard doing out in these timberlands?"

"Boy like spirit dog much," said the Indian.

"Yes, I see." Pa chewed on his lips thoughtfully. "But he's not a spirit dog, Cadje. He's real."

"He spirit dog," Cadje insisted. "He save boy from spirit world. Big widowmaker fall on boy. Spirit dog jump and shove him away."

Corky had been listening quietly. Now he saw his chance to make sure Pa would appreciate Shinglebolt.

"Pa, that's right!" he cried, leaving Shinglebolt to walk toward his father. "That big branch was huge—bigger'n most trees. I never even heard it falling. But Shinglebolt leaped out of the woods and knocked me out of the way! He saved my life, Pa!" Corky threw a fond glance at the dog, who was shaking himself again.

"That old branch would've squashed me to a flapjack! He's a real smart dog, Pa. He follows me everywhere."

Pa scratched his beard and stared at the St. Bernard thoughtfully. "I suppose you and Cadje haven't eaten. Let's get over to the cook shanty and see if Gus is still there to fill you up with something. Cadje, why don't you go tell Gus to fire up the stove, while I take this young rascal to my quarters and figure how to bunk him tonight."

Cadje nodded and padded off up the dark path.

A voice spoke from behind Corky. "Mr. Barden, I get marsh feathers for boy's bed."

"Why, that would be very nice, Elroy." Pa's voice was soft and gentle.

Corky turned to see who spoke. The flickering lantern light revealed a strange face, twisted and pulled down on the left side, with the left eye missing. Saliva dribbled down the man's chin on the loose-hanging side, but the right side of his face was grinning.

"Nice pony you got there, son," the man said, nodding toward Shinglebolt.

Corky smiled uncertainly, trying not to look at the ugly side of the face.

Pa put his arm around Corky's slender shoulders, and holding the lantern ahead of them, guided Corky up the path toward camp. Shinglebolt trotted at their heels, water dripping from his tail and chest.

Corky whispered, "What's the matter with that man?"

"You mean Elroy?" Pa sighed. "He was my best lumberjack. Two years ago last spring he was breaking a rollway for me, and he went down the long chute with the logs. We found him at the bottom, his head crushed between two logs. It's a miracle he lived. You see what it did to his face. It also injured his mind. Elroy's like a child now."

Corky looked up into Pa's sad face. "You mean he's crazy?" he whispered.

"No, no, not that. It's just that he isn't smart, though he used to be. Most of these shanty boys can't read or write. But Elroy could, before his accident. Not anymore, though." Pa shook his head. "Now he works as chore boy and handyman. Elroy is a good man. You needn't be afraid of him."

"That's the bunkhouse over there." Pa pointed to a long black shape they were passing. We'll show you around tomorrow."

A short distance farther on they arrived at a log cabin. "This is my winter home," Pa said.

As Pa held the lantern high, Corky saw that the logs stopped at the eaves, and boards were used for the gables and roof, which was covered with tar paper. Inside, Pa hung the lantern on a nail. Corky stared about him at what seemed to be a small store. There was a desk covered with two open ledger books. The log walls were nearly hidden by shelves holding tins of tobacco, socks, boots, mackinaw shirts, and tools.

Corky squinted. There didn't seem to be any bed.

Pa explained. "This is the camp store where the men buy things they need. Back here is my quarters." He opened a plank door, and they stepped into a pleasant room. A bed made of rough lumber was built into one corner. It was neatly made with a colorful quilt coverlet. Nearly covering the rough board floor was the huge oval braided rug which Corky remembered once had covered the floor of their parlor in Muskegon. In another corner was a familiar rocking chair. Corky remembered it well. When he was little and had an ear ache, Mama had cuddled him in her lap and rocked him to sleep in that very chair. Cupboards and bookshelves were heaped with books. A round oak table was surrounded by four straight chairs. Corky looked at his father, smiling. "This is really nice, Pa."

"I'm glad you like it, son. Let's wash up now, and go fill your innards with some good chow. You haven't tasted cooking until you eat Gus's."

Shinglebolt grunted and rose as they came out the door, and he padded along behind them on the way to the cook shack.

The cook shanty was the largest building in camp. The huge dining room took up most of the building, but Pa and Corky entered the kitchen section. Cadje was already seated at a small table, eating. Gus, the cook, was a small, gray-bearded man who bounced around his kitchen in high spirits. As he shook hands with Corky, he was pinching Corky's arm with his free hand.

"A winter of my cooking and you'll have some meat on those bones, son," he said. "It's high time you spent a winter with us! Look what that town-living in Muskegon does to a fellow—keeps you gant and puny."

Corky's lower lip pushed out. He didn't like being called gant and puny, but the cook didn't notice. Already Gus had turned back to his big cast iron range. Wonderful odors filled the kitchen, reminding Corky of dear Aunt Phoebe's food. Corky cleaned a plate of ham and eggs, sopping the thick yellow yolk with flaky biscuits. Just as he thought he could eat not one more crumb, Gus set a wedge-shaped slab of prune cake before him. Oh, delicious prune cake, moist and dark, just like Aunt Phoebe's! He found room for that though he feared he would pop the waist button on his pants.

When they arrived back at Pa's room, they found a bed already made for Corky in the corner opposite Pa's bed.

"Good old Elroy," murmured Pa. "He's really a good soul."

Poor Elroy with the lopsided face and addled brain had constructed Corky's bed with hemlock boughs and cedar strips, topped off with soft marsh "feathers," actually marsh hay, Pa said. The bed was made up with quilts, and there was even a grain sack stuffed with marsh feathers for a pillow.

Corky was worn out. He wasted no time climbing into the new bed. The clean aroma of cedar spread about him. "I never slept in a perfumey bed before," he grinned.

Pa laughed. "It's a nice clean smell, don't you think? It's the cedar that you smell, but it's not there to please your nose. Cedar helps keep away bedbugs."

Corky jumped up quickly, making a face. "Bedbugs! Ugh!"

"No bedbugs here," Pa chuckled. "But in the big bunkhouse where the shanty boys sleep, they can be a problem."

Relieved, Corky climbed back in bed, and Shinglebolt stretched out on the floor beside him. Was Pa going to let him stay? He wanted to ask, but decided he'd better just wait and see. Closing his eyes, Corky rolled onto his side so one arm could dangle off the bed to touch Shinglebolt's furry shoulder.

Chapter 5
The "Mess" Hall

A foghorn blast rattled the windows and bounced, echoing, through the treetops. Corky sat up in bed, blinking and confused, until he saw Pa stepping into his trousers and ignoring the racket.

"What's the noise, Pa?"

Pa pulled on his checkered shirt and laughed. "So the Gabriel woke you up, huh? That's our rise-and-shine horn to get everybody up. Elroy really blows that horn, doesn't he?"

Corky rubbed his eyes. It was still dark outside. They really got up early here. He reached over the edge of his bed to pat Shinglebolt, but the dog was gone.

"Where's Shinglebolt?" he cried, jumping out of bed.

"He had to go out. About half an hour ago he came to my bed and nudged my arm. When I opened my eyes he whined and went to the door, so I knew he wanted out. He's a well-trained dog, son."

They dressed quickly. A hasty splash with cold water from the basin on the table was their morning clean-up. The frosty air made getting into warm clothes more important than a thorough washing. Corky grinned to think how Aunt Tishia would have apoplexy if she knew how shanty men lived when they got off in the woods!

As they stepped outside, Corky looked for Shinglebolt. He whistled and called, but the shaggy dog didn't come. Shinglebolt wouldn't leave, would he? They were friends.

"It's time for breakfast," Pa said. "We'll go over to the cook shanty. Maybe the dog has followed the boys over there."

As they walked, Pa pointed out the blacksmith shop, the tinker shop, the stable, barn, and granary buildings, all at the edge of the clearing which was the logging camp. Corky murmured politely, but he was too worried about Shinglebolt to be much interested in the camp at the moment.

Several shanty boys ambled behind Corky and Pa, heading for breakfast. As they approached the dining end of the cook shack, a gigantic roar blasted from inside. Loud crashes and bellowing followed.

Everyone scrambled through the doorway into the mess hall and stared. Corky gasped at the sight.

Four long tables, each covered with shiny green oilcloth, filled the huge room. Two of the tables were set for breakfast with platters of steaming flapjacks, pitchers of black strap molasses, gravy and coffee, and more platters of meat and biscuits. But the other two tables were a shambles! Plates, spilled syrup, and coffee littered the floor. On top of one wrecked table stood Shinglebolt, wolfing down a platter of fried pork. The cook, Gus, his face livid, crouched beside the table roaring and swinging a broom at the gigantic dog's hindquarters. With each swat of the broom, Shinglebolt grunted and swayed, yet never missed a mouthful.

"Great Scott!" bellowed Pa, lurching into the fracas. He grabbed the St. Bernard by his long mane hair and began tugging at him.

Corky leaped toward the tussle, sliding on the slippery floor. Just as he fell, sprawling through sticky syrup, Corky saw the table overturn as Shinglebolt was pulled off. Tin plates, forks, and knives clattered to the floor, accompanied by the sound of shattering platters and coffee mugs.

The shanty boys, who had stood aghast and gaping just inside the doorway, surged forward, whooping, but stopped short as they saw Julius Barden, flat on his back, the monster dog standing over him, licking syrup from his flushed cheeks. The woodsmen hooted and whistled, slapping their mackinaw trousers in glee.

Because of Shinglebolt, the shanty boys were one hour late getting into the woods that day. Not wanting to lose their masterful cook, some of the men helped clean up the ruined dining hall, while others helped Gus prepare another breakfast.

Pa took Corky and Shinglebolt back to his cabin. It seemed best to get the dog out of Gus's sight at once. Corky's stomach was a tight knot as he wondered what Pa would do to him and Shinglebolt. They

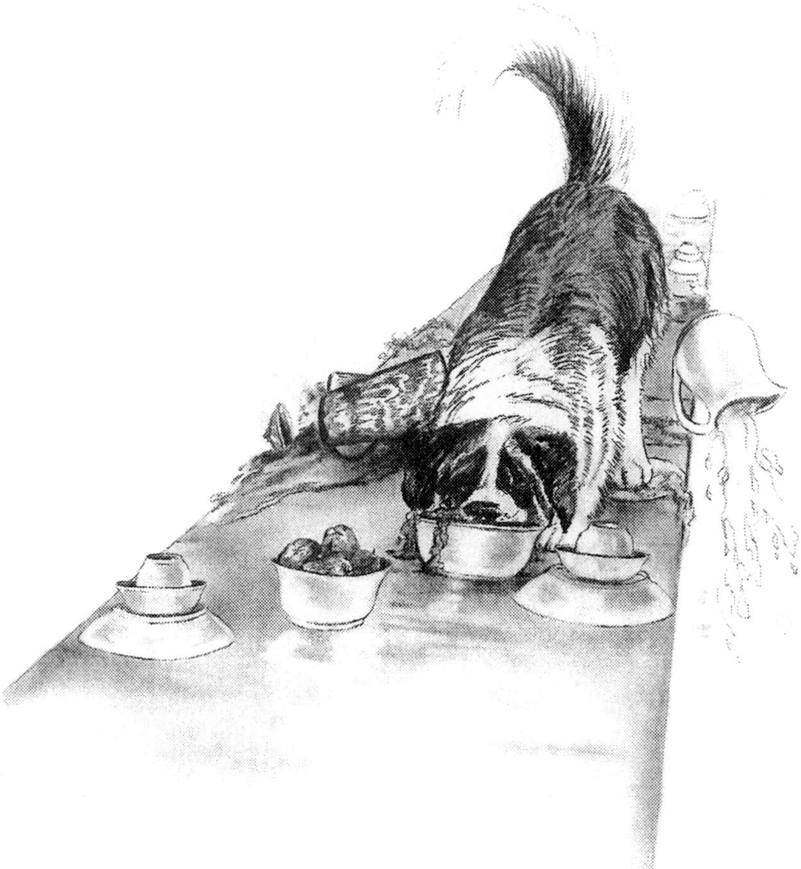

stepped into the first room, the camp store, and Pa quickly shut the door behind them.

Then he turned sternly to Corky. "Son, when did you last feed that dog?"

Corky blinked. Food for Shinglebolt? He'd been so excited about getting here, he hadn't thought about it. At last he remembered. Ashamed, he whispered, "Yesterday morning we gave him a beaver carcass."

"Well, crowfeathers, boy!" yelled Pa. "No wonder he got into trouble! He's a big dog, and he needs lots of food. He walked a long way following your canoe. That takes grub."

Corky hung his head and felt terrible. He sure hadn't been a good friend to Shinglebolt. He blinked back tears and kept his head down, not wanting Pa to see him bawling like a baby. He heard Pa moving about the store, but he dared not look up until he conquered his tears.

"Corky," Pa's voice sounded gentle. "Here's the solution to keeping Shinglebolt out of trouble."

Corky looked up and gulped in horror. Pa was holding a rifle.

"Pa, you wouldn't!" cried Corky. "Please don't shoot Shinglebolt!" Now the tears spilled out of Corky's eyes as he stared into Pa's face.

At first Pa looked puzzled. Then he understood. "Thunderation, son, I wouldn't shoot that fine dog! This gun is for you. With it, you'll learn how to hunt game to feed his big appetite. Within a mile of camp you can hunt beaver and coon, and when you get to be a good hunter, maybe you can sneak up on a deer."

"Oh, Pa, a gun for me?" Now Corky's eyes shown with tears of happiness. He stroked the shiny golden brass frame with his index finger.

"Sure, boy," Pa smiled. "You're old enough to learn how to handle a rifle safely and realize it's a dangerous weapon. I don't want you mistaking any of my shanty boys for a deer or a bear. But to get meat on the table, a gun is necessary up here in the woods. There's no butcher shop down the street where we can buy meat. We must hunt it down, shoot it, dress it, and get it back to Gus and his kitchen in order to feed these hungry loggers. That's Cadje's big job during the logging season. Now you must do the same for your tail-wagging monster there."

Both Pa and Corky grinned at Shinglebolt, who was sitting politely on his haunches with his tail thumping eagerly.

"You can go out hunting with Cadje, and you'll be learning from the master hunter," Pa said. "But not today. I've got to send him down to Muskegon to carry word to your Aunt Tishia that you're safe, and that you're going to stay with me for awhile. Tishia will be having the purple vapors with worry. She probably has most of Muskegon searching for you."

"Oh, Pa! I can stay?" Corky cried. "Oh, thanks, Pa!" Corky threw himself at Pa and hugged him around the chest.

Pa lifted Corky off his feet in a big hug. "Say, you're growing up. Pretty soon I won't be able to heave you around like I used to," he said.

Corky stepped back and looked up at Pa. "Can I always be with you from now on, Pa? Please?"

Pa cleared his throat and rubbed his short red beard. "Well, we don't have to make any quick decisions, Corky. But the fact is, you must get an education. You have a lot of learning to do yet."

"But, Pa," Corky pleaded, "I can learn everything I want to know right here in the woods with you and Cadje."

Pa sat down on the long wooden bench and studied his boots before answering. "You're right in saying you can learn a lot here in the woods. All about logging, survival, and the natural surroundings here. But this section of woods is only a speck in this big world we live in. And logging is just one way of making a living. I want you to learn about the rest of the world, and about other ways of making a living."

"But I want to live here and be a lumberman just like you," Corky insisted.

"I'd be very happy to be partners with you someday, son. But as I've told you before, I want a smart partner. Whoever becomes partner with me will have to have a good education."

Corky sighed and kicked at a crack in the rough flooring. "When do I have to go back?"

"You can stay here for a short while and see how our logging operation works. You can get to know what shanty boys are like and what they do," said Pa. "But then you must go back to school and keep learning everything you must know."

Corky held on to the thought that he could stay for "a short while." In the meantime he'd try to figure out something.

Pa heaved himself from the bench. "I know you're anxious to try out that rifle. I'll try to get things cleared up this morning so I can take you into the woods this afternoon to get Shinglebolt his supper. That breakfast he just had should hold him for a few hours."

Corky started to hang his head again, but then he saw that Pa's eyes were flashing with amusement. Corky rolled his eyes, and they laughed together. It *had* been a wild sight—Shinglebolt moving down that long table devouring food, just like a locomotive chugging down the track.

Pa showed Corky how the rifle worked. It was a Henry, forty-four caliber rifle with a tubular magazine extending the full length of the twenty-four inch barrel.

"The magazine will hold fifteen of these rimfire cartridges," Pa explained. "It's really an exciting gun. With this one motion of this lever, the fired cartridge ejects, the hammer cocks, and you're all re-loaded." Pa closed the breech with a flourish. "Beautiful, eh?"

Corky watched, fascinated, as Pa flipped the lever and opened and closed the breech once again.

"Cadje is a real master with a Henry. I've seen him get off thirty shots in one minute, with re-loading once.

"But no cartridges, yet, Corky. Just carry the empty gun around, practice sighting it, get so you know its balance, so it's almost a third arm. You and that rifle will be together every time you're out of camp.

"Now I'm going back to the cook house to see if I can calm down Gus. You go over to the stable and ask Frenchie to take a piece of harness leather and make a harness for your dog. There's going to be times when we'll have to tie up Shinglebolt—at least until we can be certain he'll stay away from the cook house. And for Pete's sake, keep that dog out of Gus's sight for a few days!"

"Yes, sir," Corky grinned. As the door shut behind Pa, he sat down on the plank floor, his left hand stroking Shinglebolt, and his right hand caressing his beautiful new forty-four. His chest ached, he was so full of happiness.

Mid-afternoon, Pa and Corky started down the two-track tote road into the forest. Shinglebolt ambled along, sporting a new brown harness contraption over his front shoulders. At first the giant dog had rolled and scratched at this strange thing sticking to him, but after Corky petted him and praised his handsome appearance, Shinglebolt accepted the harness with dignity.

Corky carried his gun proudly, although there were no cartridges in the magazine. "I'll do the shooting today, son," Pa said. "You don't just get a gun and go blasting away. There's much to learn. But when you see something you would want to shoot, go ahead and aim and see if you can get it in your sights and keep it there. You'll get an idea how fast you have to be, and how careful not to raise your gun at just any movement or sound. Even when you're several miles from camp, away from our operations, you must remember that something moving might be a timber cruiser inspecting a section of land, or even an itinerant preacher going through the woods to a wedding or a burying. These woods aren't so wild and deserted as they used to be. Each year there seem to be more and more people moving through, heading farther north, especially to the Big Rapids. After you get some experience hunting, you'll be able to get a deer at even a long distance." Pa chuckled. "A fat deer carcass might satisfy this dog's appetite for a couple days anyway."

They climbed a steep ridge and moved along, Pa instructing Corky all the way. "This time of year, because of mating season, the buck deer are getting pretty gant. From now until early spring does are better. And remember, almost always the older deer are fatter than the young ones."

Corky nodded, trying hard to remember these things.

As they picked their way through the dense timber, climbing over fallen half-decayed trees, Pa pointed out different kinds of trees— the hemlocks, whose tops, he said, always pointed toward the rising sun. "Once you can see the tops of hemlock trees, you'll always know which way is east. Greenhorns get lost in the woods real easy because they think they'll tell direction by the sun. In tall timber the sun's hard to find. Remember, just look for hemlock trees if you get confused. They're a beautiful tree, very graceful, but no good for lumber. Hemlock wood splinters and warps, and the knots are like stones. They ruin saws and axes. Hemlock isn't even good for firewood because it throws terrible sparks."

As they jumped across a tiny stream Pa pointed out the tamarack trees drooping over the creek bed. He explained that tamaracks were strange trees in that they shed their needles at wintertime just as leafy trees do. "Tamarack roots grow deep into the moist soil, seeking a firm foundation. These root fibers are strong as a shoemaker's waxed thread. Indians always have used tamarack roots for their thread, especially in binding together their birchbark canoes."

"Ho, look here!" cried Pa, as a fluttering blur of brown flew off. "We've got our first catch without firing a shot." It was a passenger pigeon, freshly killed by the hawk which they had frightened off. "Feel it. It's still warm, so you know it's a fresh kill."

Corky touched the warm feathers and nodded.

"Of course, when you're hunting game for Shinglebolt, you won't have to be so particular about meat. We humans have to have fresh meat, but animals thrive on meat that would be too tainted for us. Now, a two-day old deer carcass would be quite a delicacy to Shinglebolt here, but people's innards don't work that well."

Corky toted the pigeon while they tramped on. They came to a valley filled with black ash trees of great height but with slender trunks, so different from the thick-trunked white pine surrounding the valley. Pa explained that black ash wood was tough and elastic. After being soaked, the wood could be bent and pounded. The annual growth rings would separate into flexible slats, much in demand for barrel hoops. "The Indians use black ash for their utensils, and.."

Pa broke off suddenly. Before Corky could raise his own gun, his ears pounded with the echoing crack of Pa's rifle.

"I think I got her!" Pa shouted as he sped off along the slope.

Corky crashed and stumbled behind. Pa had his knife out, ready to skin the white-tailed deer, a fat doe, by the time Corky jogged up, panting.

"Now we're in jim dandy shape," Pa grinned. "This ought to keep Shinglebolt out of the cook house for a few days."

With a deep bark, Shinglebolt agreed, and the brown drooping eyes fastened on the fallen deer with eagerness.

"I think he knows it's for him, Pa," said Corky.

"Well, now we've done the easy part. I'll show you how to dress out a deer carcass. That's not so hard, either. The hard part comes in carrying it back to camp. We'll split up the carcass and each carry some, but I sure don't know what you'll do if you're out this far alone and get a deer." Pa's sharp hunting knife flicked quickly through the cleaning. "Of course, once snow covers the ground, you can skin the carcass and set it on the hide and drag it. Even then, it's hard work until you find a cleared trail."

"Why couldn't Shinglebolt help carry meat?" asked Corky. "He's bigger and stronger than I am, and after all, it's for him."

Pa paused, looking thoughtfully at Corky, then at the giant, panting dog. "You may have a good idea there. I believe that dog could carry a sixty or seventy pound load on his back. The Indians use dogs for carrying packs, and their dogs are midgets compared to this monster."

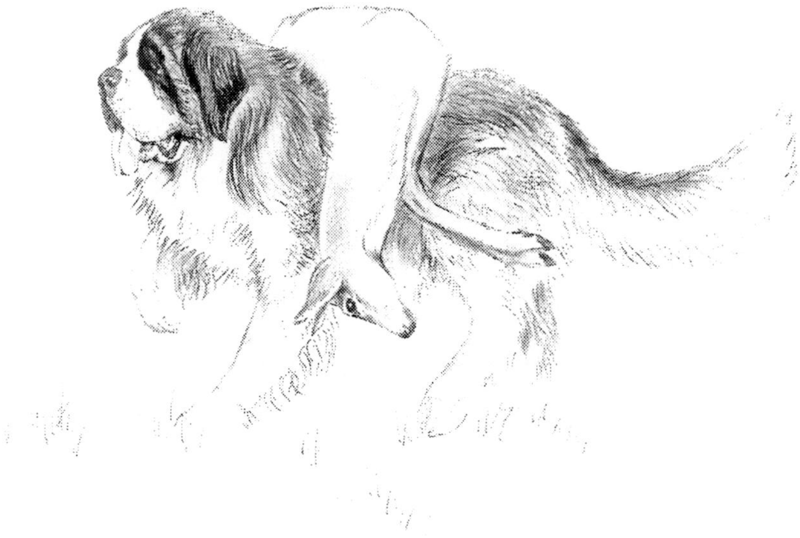

Chapter 6
Four Peach Pies!

And so it was that the big St. Bernard returned to the logging camp carrying his next day's meal across his shoulders. Corky walked alongside to steady the load, but Shinglebolt's shoulders bore the weight. Though Pa carried over half the meat, it was the dog who got the attention as they trooped into camp. Shinglebolt lifted high his huge white paws, very much aware of admiring eyes upon him.

"Pretty smart dog!" called Frenchie from the stable. "Bring him back tomorrow, and I fix a better back pack for him."

Corky waved, nodding, and grinned triumphantly until they came to the ice house where perishables were stored, right beside the cook shanty. Wearing a long white apron, and grasping a heavy iron skillet, Gus leaned against the cook house door, glaring.

"We got the shaggy beast some food, Gus," Pa spoke cheerfully, ignoring the cook's sullen look. "Now he'll stay out of your bailiwick."

Gus only grunted and disappeared inside his kitchen.

That night as Corky slid into his pungent-smelling bed, he remembered The Haunt, and the mysterious things the old man had said. "Pa, on our way up river, Cadje and I stopped off at The Haunt's." Corky paused, thinking Pa would take it from there and explain about the old hermit.

"Yes," Pa mumbled. "Cadje told me."

"He's a strange old man, isn't he?" Corky prompted.

Corky's only answer was a grunt, as Pa struggled to remove a boot. Silence followed as Pa finished undressing, blew out the lamp, and crawled into his bed.

Corky spoke into the darkness. "How come The Haunt knew Mama?"

There was a loud creak. Corky suspected Pa had suddenly sat up in bed.

"Huh! What did the old man say to make you think he knew Mama?" Pa asked.

Now Corky was afraid he'd pushed the subject too far, but he stumbled on. "He told me what Mama said when she was dying."

A big sigh came from Pa's bed. "Oh, that. The old man gets a bit dotty in the head sometimes. Don't let him fret you."

Corky opened his mouth to say more, but thought better of it. "Good night, Pa," he said.

"Good night, son."

For the next two days Cadje was away at Muskegon, and Pa was busy getting the logging operations underway for the new season. Corky and Shinglebolt wandered around the camp buildings, getting acquainted with the layout of "Barden's Slashing," as Pa's camp was called. They spent a lot of time with Frenchie at the stables where Corky helped brush down horses, clean out stalls, and oil harness, getting everything ready for the long, cold logging season ahead. Animals and equipment had to work perfectly, Frenchie warned. A harness or chain breaking on a horse-drawn sleigh piled high with logs could mean injury or death to shanty boys.

Sometimes Corky followed Charlie, the handyman, about on his chores. Charlie said he was called a "bull cook," which meant he was a general "fixer" in lumber camp language.

Evenings, Pa showed Corky how to load and unload the Henry rifle, and how to keep it clean. He taught Corky the safe way to carry the weapon when crawling over fallen trees. After some pestering by Corky, Pa finally allowed him to carry two cartridges in his coat pocket. "But not in the gun, understand? Not yet. I want you to do some hunting with Cadje before you go out alone with a loaded gun."

Whenever Corky had to go to the ice house for another chunk of Shinglebolt's venison, he tried to schedule his errand during the hour just before meal time, hoping that Gus would be busy cooking. Corky didn't wish to chance an encounter between Gus and Shinglebolt.

Shinglebolt was so friendly, he'd probably run right up to the cook and slobber all over him.

Cadje returned from his trip to Muskegon, reporting that Aunt Tishia was furious. "She most mad at you, boss," he warned. "She mad at me because I come to Muskegon alone, but she most mad because you not send boy back. I get away from skinny aunt fast! Afraid she come back with me."

"You bring her here, Cadje, and it's the last bringing you'll ever do!" Pa laughed. "Besides, the shanty boys wouldn't stand for it. They say a woman is bad luck in a logging camp."

Cadje grunted. "*That* woman bad luck anywhere."

"Well, Cadje, are you too tired to go out and get us a deer today? The men have been eating side pork while you've been gone, and Gus says he wants some venison."

"I tired in Muskegon. Too much houses, too much people. Never tired in woods."

"Good. How about taking Corky with you and showing him how you do it? I promised him you'd teach him to be a good hunter. He has to learn how to keep that dog fed."

Cadje agreed, saying they would leave at noon. Corky hurried back to the cabin to get his rifle. He sat cross-legged in front of the cabin on a flat pine slab, completely absorbed in polishing the Henry and daydreaming about sighting his gun on a deer. He didn't notice when Shinglebolt wakened from a snooze and trotted off toward the cook shanty, his moist black nose twitching and sniffing.

The commotion from the direction of the cook shack brought Corky out of his thoughts. With a sinking feeling he saw that Shinglebolt was gone. "Oh, no," he moaned, jumping to his feet and racing toward the noise.

"Four peach pies! Four peach pies!" Gus was screeching over and over. As Corky dashed up, the bearded cook howled at him, "I'll kill that dog! I'm gonna kill him!"

Charlie stood beside Gus, staring dolefully at an overturned pie on the ground, and three empty pie tins scattered about.

"Your pa got to make a choice!" Gus yelled at Corky. "That dog goes, or I go!"

It was simple to see what had happened. There was a wide slab shelf built onto the outside of the kitchen window. Four steaming peach pies had been set there by the cook to cool. Their drifting aroma must have attracted Shinglebolt, and he had disgraced himself again.

Corky tried to think of something to say other than just "I'm sorry," which sounded pretty weak. Before he could say anything, a terrible snarling and growling uproar came from the woods behind the cook house. The shrieks and grunts grew to a higher pitch as Corky stood motionless, dumbfounded, his mouth agape. Cadje tore past the cook house in the direction of the screeching, fighting clamor, his rifle up and ready.

Cadje's racing into the woods brought Corky into action, and he pounded after the silently running Indian. Then the whole clearing came to life, and Gus, Charlie and several shanty boys followed Corky.

As Corky ran, the snarling uproar grew louder for a moment, then suddenly ceased. Corky stopped still in surprise. Charlie, barreling along behind, whacked into Corky with a thud, and they both tumbled to the ground. Gus and the following shanty boys leaped over them and tore on. Above the heavy breathing of the running men could be heard a deep, steady growling.

Charlie pulled Corky to his feet, and they hurried toward the growling. Ahead, the shanty boys huddled close together exclaiming, "Did you ever!" and "I'll be hornswoggled!" Their surprised rumblings grew until they drowned out the growling.

Corky pushed his way through the circle of men. He saw Cadje scratching his stocking cap, his head cocked to one side, puzzled. Then the boy saw Shinglebolt, his four legs planted far apart, the fur down his center back standing straight up. Beneath him on the ground lay a dark lump.

Cadje broke into a broad grin and rubbed his brown cheek bone. "Spirit dog mighty hunter. He do what no other dog do."

With a gleeful whoop, Charlie whacked Gus a mighty thump on the back. There's your pie thief, Gus. I always said your pies was sweeter'n honey, and bears shore like honey." He doubled over guffawing and slapping his thighs.

A hulking blond they called "Swede" looked down at Corky, grinning.

"What is it!" Corky cried. "I don't understand."

The man pointed a muscular arm toward the unmoving furry mass on the ground. "Black bear. Big one, too. Old 'Three-Paws' we

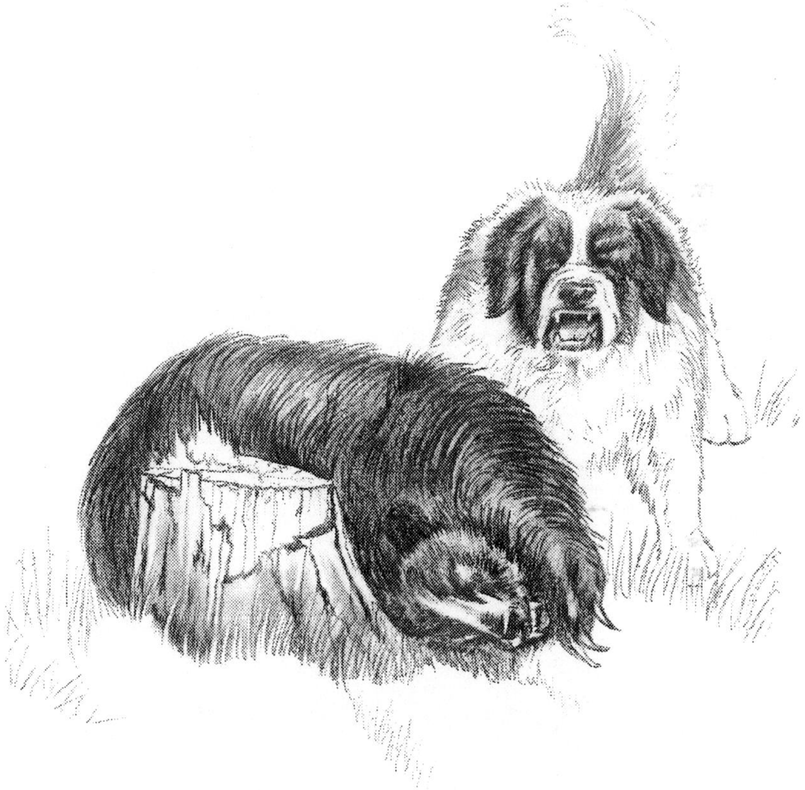

named him. He's been raidin' around camp lately. He musta lost that paw in a bear trap once. Old Three-Paws musta gone after Gus's peach pies and your dog chased him off and kilt him, all by hisself. Never heard tell of one dog killin' a bear!"

Chapter 7
Cork Pine and Pemmican

More than anything else, woodsmen admire a brave act. The river hog who dances across jammed logs, balancing himself with his peavey, is their hero. At night in the bunkhouse they sing songs about the brave river men, those who survived, and especially, those who did not. They tell stories about fearless Billy Barrelton and Jack Monroe, who approached danger head on and met death.

Now the shanty boys had another hero—a peculiar-looking giant dog, said by Cadje to be a spirit dog. The huge dog had attacked a black bear four times his size. In less than five minutes the dog had broken the bear's neck. Shinglebolt had lost some patches of fur and bore claw marks on his muzzle, but he suffered no serious injury. This extraordinary feat would entertain the shanty boys for many a cold winter night to come.

The size of the bear was impressive. Cadje and Charlie skinned the fur off carefully. "I tan it for you," Cadje promised Corky. "It make big blanket."

After they'd dressed out the bear carcass, Gus weighed the meat and it came to over four hundred pounds. Bear were fattest in October, having gorged themselves throughout autumn to store up body fat for their winter hibernation which started in November. Later, Gus said that he got twenty gallons of bear oil from the carcass, something of a record.

Nearly every day Corky and Shinglebolt trailed through the woods with Cadje. Corky learned how to track game, and how to find his way in the unending forest. The stands of hardwood trees, except for the oak, were now barren, their brittle leaves smothering the ground. As November progressed, the air grew crisp. Pa and the shanty boys hoped for snow.

Few of the men were cutting big timber yet because it was too difficult to haul the monstrous logs to the banking grounds on the river's edge, where they would be stored until spring. Snow turned the ground into a slippery floor upon which the logs could be slid and dragged. Pa had most of the shanty boys working in the section of last year's slashing, cutting shinglebolts from the thigh-high stumps left from last year's cutting. Corky didn't like to go to that part of the forest, where only ugly stumps and piles of brush from treetops remained.

Once Corky had asked Pa what he would do when he had logged off the whole forest.

That afternoon Pa took Corky to the banking grounds, a flat cleared plateau which ended in a sandy cliff dropping off to the river, over one hundred feet below. From this height the river looked like a small creek. Pa put his arm around Corky's shoulder and pointed across the river, far below. The opposite river bank was low, not many feet above the river surface. Beyond that as far as Corky could see, clear to the horizon, stretched a green blanket over the earth. There before his eyes lay an endless blue-green valley of white pine trees.

"How many years would it take us to cut all those trees, son?" asked Pa. "And those are only what you can see from here, say, maybe ten or fifteen miles of pine. That timber there stretches north for hundreds of miles. It covers the whole northern half of Michigan! Don't worry about the trees. There will always be plenty of trees.

"The world is begging for those trees you see out there. Wood is needed to build houses, barns, ships, wagons, and factories. Out West across the Mississippi River there aren't many trees. The settlers there need the lumber from these trees." Pa swung his arm toward the far horizon. "That green blanket of pine trees is green gold to me and other lumbermen. It's more valuable and will bring more money than all the yellow gold out in California."

Corky could understand that people did need lumber. Still, a sadness always gripped him when he saw a cork pine plunge to earth. The giant cork pine was most prized by the lumbermen. It was the king of all the white pine, sometimes towering one hundred seventy feet toward the open sky. Its deeply furrowed dark gray trunk grew stout and straight, bearing not a single branch three-quarters of the way up. No branches meant no knots in the clear, creamy white wood.

Corky had been nicknamed after the cork pine. His real name was Howard Clark Barden. "Corky" was the name Pa had given him when he was just a babe. Pa said he called him "Corky" because he was such a prize, just as a giant cork pine is a prize. Corky felt a kinship with these great tall trees, and he was proud to share their name.

Beneath the great cork pines there was no brush and no young trees, only a soft carpet of cones and needles. The wood of the cork pine was light in weight, making its logs float high in the water. Some of the larger logs were five feet in diameter. Pa said these bigger cork pines were nearly three hundred years old. This was what made Corky flinch when one of the great trees was brought to earth. It seemed almost sinful for men to destroy a living tree which Pa said had been a forty-foot high youngster at the time the pilgrims landed at Plymouth. The tree had been of great size when George Washington was born. It had lived through all sorts of history, and had survived storms and droughts. *But it couldn't survive the axes and saws of the lumbermen like Pa,* Corky thought.

He hoped that the fine lumber from the cut-down cork pines would be used in some grand building, a church or a museum. In this way, its wood might survive another three hundred years. Or better yet, Corky hoped the cork pine boards might be used in a graceful swift Clipper ship, which would sail to China or the Spice Islands. That would be more fitting than if its lumber were used for a chicken coop or a backyard outbuilding.

Another part of lumbering that Corky disliked was the ugliness created by cutting trees. The cut-over sections were barren stretches of land, pock-marked with dark tree stumps and piles of brown, dead foliage. Pa said the pine stumps never would rot away because they contained so much pitch. Corky thought it sad to think of those huge dead stumps standing there forever, almost whispering, "Once we were a beautiful forest." Because of the closely spaced, deep-rooted stumps, the land couldn't be cultivated by farmers. Lumbered-off land became a wasteland.

Corky preferred to wander through untouched parts of the forest. He grew accustomed to the perpetual greenish light in the woods, where the treetops hoarded the sunlight. Once the sun filtered through pine needles, it became green sunbeams. He loved to hear the wind whistling through the overhead pine needles, and the pleasant crunch made by dry needles beneath his boots.

When Corky happened upon an open, swampy meadow, his spirits leaped with the excitement of coming upon something new and bright. He and Shinglebolt raced and tumbled in the dry swamp grass, tossing their heads in the rare sunlight.

One afternoon while Corky hunted with Cadje, a few snowflakes sifted through the trees, dropping softly about them.

"Bon!" the Indian grunted. "Good we get snow."

Cadje taught Corky some ways of getting along in snow and freezing weather. "Before, we not build fire because it dry. Maybe start big woods fire. Once snow on ground, can build fire. Fire keep you from freezing. Carry matches, toujours. Always."

The Indian promised to show Corky how to make snowshoes for getting around in deep snow. He showed him how he could make temporary snowshoes if he were caught out in the woods in a sudden, deep snowfall. It was simple. You just fastened a broad cedar branch to each foot. Cadje said it would keep you from sinking into the deep drifts. He told Corky that if he got lost or hurt in the woods, he should bury himself under cedar boughs for protection and warmth.

One day Cadje showed Corky how to make pemmican, the food Cadje always carried with him when out hunting. A small amount of pemmican was light to carry and very nourishing. First, Cadje cut animal fat into small pieces and began cooking them slowly in his big iron skillet. While the fat was melting, he took a large piece of dried meat called "Jerky" and pounded it until it crumbled into fine granules. Next he poured the melted fat over the pounded jerky. Cadje explained that the secret of good pemmican was to combine the melted fat and meat granules in equal amounts. The finished mixture resembled sausage. Cadje packed a deerskin pouch tightly with pemmican and handed it to Corky.

"Carry with you when in woods. Pemmican and matches. You will be not hungry, not cold."

Corky didn't like the taste of pemmican. But by and by, when he and Cadje stayed out in the woods for a long time, he learned to appreciate having it to eat. It was better than nothing.

At last, toward the end of November the camp awakened one morning to find several inches of welcome snow covering the ground. After breakfast Pa gave orders that the boys should quit cutting shinglebolts in the old slashing and start on the new quarter section of woods. Timber cutting would begin in earnest.

At the stable Corky watched Frenchie getting the teams harnessed and ready to head into the woods to their job of pulling the huge logs to storage at the banking grounds.

Pa stopped by the stable, his eyes sparkling. Now the real business could begin. His sandy hair curled out from under his lucky stocking cap with the peculiar green crown. Hands upon hips, he beamed down at Corky. "Do you still have those cartridges in your pocket, son?"

Corky fished in his jacket pocket and held out the two cartridges for his precious Henry.

"You can put them in your gun today, Corky. With this snowfall it should be a good day for tracking coon." Pa grinned. "Over by the swamp you might find a tasty beaver."

"Wow! Thanks Pa!" Corky exclaimed. It was a great day.

Chapter 8
Murder in the Big Woods

Corky set off in the opposite direction from the timber-cutting operations. Just before noon he discovered fresh beaver tracks, and soon after, with only one shot, he bagged a plump beaver for Shinglebolt's dinner.

Nearly every night a little more snow fell, and the temperature kept dropping. A thin sheet of ice formed on the edge of the river, and then slowly grew wider and thicker, reaching toward the middle, where the current fought to keep ice from forming. Every morning Corky helped Frenchie break ice from the livestock watering troughs.

Several times each week Corky joined Cadje to hunt. From the shrewd Indian he picked up a great deal of woodland knowledge. Now that snow covered the forest floor, Cadje taught Corky how to distinguish animal tracks. With the danger of forest fire past because of the snow blanket, it was safe to build fires and cook game they had shot. Cadje even had advice on the sort of campfire one should build.

"Make small fire. Can get close to small fire. Get warm. Big fire too hot. Keep you away. White man always make big fire." He snorted in disgust at such foolishness.

One day when Cadje and Corky were returning to camp they came upon a dome-shaped wigwam. The small round hut was formed of saplings covered with large sheets of birchbark.

"This my sweat lodge," said Cadje. "I come here to clean my spirit." He pulled aside the blanket-flap doorway, and Corky peered inside. The round hut was empty except for a cast iron tray filled with round stones. Cadje explained that he heated the rocks, then sprinkled them with cold water to make steam, which filled the small wigwam with moist hot air.

"When spirit sink low, I come here," the Indian said. "Sweat lodge lift spirit tall and strong."

In the crisp air sounds traveled a long way. Even in camp Corky could hear the far off whacks of razor-sharp axes felling timber nearly a mile away. The thud of a falling giant pine sounded every few minutes.

The shanty boys returned to camp at dusk, bone tired and hungry. After twelve hours of hard labor in the woods they fell at their evening meal with gusto, devouring huge amounts of pork, beans, and potatoes, along with thick slices of Gus's bread smothered in sticky, dark molasses. When Corky figured they could eat no more, the men began on their dessert, which often meant several large portions of gingerbread and a bowl of rice pudding.

After eating, the men retired to the bunkhouse where decks of cards were brought out. Euchre and Old Sledge were their favorite card games. The men took turns, one at a time, at the grindstone outside the bunkhouse. There, beneath a swaying kerosene lantern, each shanty boy honed his ax to a fine sharp edge.

Usually two or three shanty boys sat on a nearby slab bench, waiting their turn at the grindstone. Corky liked to sit with them, sniffing the sweet smoke from their pipes and listening to their stories. Three of the men claimed to have seen a Hodag. Corky nodded solemnly to their stories, knowing that if he showed he didn't believe, they would shut him out of their comradeship.

It seemed that it was only the Hodag which they took seriously. As lovers of exaggeration and tall tales, the shanty boys had a host of other mythical animals which they talked about. But with these creatures, their eyes danced merrily, and Corky knew it was all right to laugh.

They talked of the strange creature, the Gyascutus, which sort of resembled a deer, though it had the ears of a rabbit and the teeth of a lion. It was said to have legs which folded within themselves like a folding telescope. This was to their advantage for grazing on hillsides. You saw the Gyascutus, they said, only after being bitten by a rattlesnake.

The shanty boys whooped and slapped their knees over the Goofus Bird, which flew backwards because he didn't care where he was going, but he liked to see where he'd been.

Corky's favorite was another bird, called the Gillygaloo. The men said that the Gillygaloo nested on hillsides; it laid square eggs so the eggs wouldn't roll away downhill. Gillgaloo eggs were greatly prized because once they were hard-boiled, the shanty boys claimed they used them as dice.

For six days out of each week the lumber camp routine continued unvaried. The far-off sounds of chopping and crashing timber echoed through the camp during the daylight hours. Sundays, the men did not go into the woods. It was their day off, but hardly a day of rest. Sunday was known as Boil-up Day. On this day the lumberjacks boiled their heavy clothes to get rid of the week's collection of lice. In the center of the bunkhouse stood a large box stove which heated the place. Large strands of hay baling wire stretched outward from the hot stove, and these wires were the drying lines upon which the wet clothes were hung. On Boil-up Day with all the wet clothes drying around the stove, steam grew so dense in the bunkhouse that one could not see the length of the large room. Corky visited the bunkhouse once on Boil-up Day and decided "never again." The stench of wet woolen clothes was awful.

Weeks sped by quickly in the woods, where there was so much to do and to see, and all of it fun. Back in Muskegon when Corky was living there with Aunt Phoebe, winters had seemed endless. He used to wonder if spring ever would come. Now the winter days flew by, bringing near the time when Pa would send him back to Muskegon. How he loved being with Pa! And there was Cadje, who was teaching him important things that Miss Swensen never could teach him. Every night after getting into bed, Pa and Corky took turns reading to each other from some of Pa's books. Pa said that if Corky would read many books, he wouldn't get so far behind in school.

"Read and learn, son," Pa said. Corky was happy to read, especially if it delayed his going back to Muskegon, to Miss Swensen and Aunt Phoebe, or worse, Aunt Tishia, and the teasing he took over being part-Indian.

It was strange that here at camp, no one ever mentioned his having Indian blood. Pa said most of the shanty boys were either Swedish or of French-Indian ancestry. Next to Pa, Cadje was the most respected man in camp. It almost seemed that here at camp it was in your favor to have Indian ancestry. The man who could survive whatever hardships Nature threw at him was the man who was well thought of. Each person was judged by what he did, not by who he was, or who his parents were. Corky thought that was the way the whole world should be.

Just being around Cadje and Pa would have made Corky happy enough, but having Shinglebolt as his companion was the molasses on the bread of Corky's new life. Shinglebolt listened to him talk, and answered with moist licks and thumping tail. Corky didn't miss boys his own age because Shinglebolt was like another boy, loving to wrestle over the ground, jump, climb hills and slide and skid back down.

As winter hurried on, it grew colder, even though the men were beginning to mention spring and the anticipated time of the river drive.

Corky was now an able hunter of game for Shinglebolt. Often by mid-morning he had filled his game pouch with a two-day supply of meat for Shinglebolt. This left them free to explore the woods. Sometimes they timed their wanderings to take them at noon to the cutting section, where men were felling timber. That way Corky could join the shanty boys in their mid-day lunch break. Corky and each of the shanty boys carried their lunch with them in a "nosebag," an oilcloth drawstring sack, which they kept tied out of their way on the back of their belts. These nosebags were filled with biscuits, cookies, doughnuts, ham and eggs, and proved much tastier than Cadje's pemmican, though Corky always carried the smaller skin bag of pemmican, too, for use in an emergency.

The shanty boys wasted no time wolfing down the contents of their nosebags. They were hungry, and it was too cold to sit still long.

As the men resumed working, Corky and Shinglebolt retired to the outskirts of the cutting operations. Corky dipped into his game pouch and brought out part of a raccoon carcass for Shinglebolt. While the dog ate, Corky watched the lumbering activities. Against the white snow and the dark tree trunks the shanty boys were a colorful sight with their blue or red woolen shirts, warm pants known as "Canadian gray," their bright-colored knit caps, many of which stretched out into long tails. Most of the men wore a bright red sash, the badge of the shanty boy. Their feet were protected with walking rubbers strapped at the ankle, and some of the men wore heavy overcoats against the frigid air.

With grunts of exertion they swung their sharp axes at the heavy trunks. As they worked, tiny icicles formed on the men's beards.

After a few weeks of watching, Corky began to understand how the timber cutting process worked. First, the sawyers and choppers cut down a huge tree. Then the trimmers took over, hacking off the branches and the top of the tree. While the long tree trunk was being sawn into sixteen-foot lengths, swampers were cutting a path from the fallen tree to the closest hauling road. There, the logs were pulled onto a "skid," made of long, heavy poles set at right angles to the road. As the logs collected high upon the skid, a man called a "scaler" recorded the number of board feet he estimated in each log. He calculated this by multiplying the length of each log by its diameter.

While still piled upon the skid, each log was branded with Pa's log mark, which was **JB**. This symbol blended the "J" and "B," Pa's initials. A heavy iron marker with this insignia was held against the cut end of each log and pounded with a sledge, leaving a depression reading "JB," branding the log as belonging to Julius Barden. During the spring when logs from dozens of camps filled the Muskegon River, logs from different owners became mixed up. At the booming grounds at the mouth of the river the men sorted the logs by reading the log marks of ownership on each log.

After being scaled and stamped, the logs were transferred onto a sleigh which would pull the load to the banking grounds. The sleigh stood on thick wooden runners shod with steel bars. The crosswise beam connecting the two sleigh runners was called a "bunk," and from the bunk rose huge spikes at either end to stick into the bottom layer of logs and keep the load from falling off. Chains were looped around each log, and horse teams pulled them from the skid onto the sleigh with the help of men wielding cant hooks.

Corky loved to watch the Sky-loader, the man who stood atop the growing load and directed the placement of each log. The Sky-loader was the highest paid man in the crew because of the danger of his position, where he could be crushed by slipping logs. A pair of horses could pull from five to fifteen logs, depending upon the logs' size. When the Sky-loader judged he had a full load, he sang out, "Scoot her to the drink, boys!" As he braced himself atop the tall load, he flicked the reins, and the horses leaned forward, straining in their harness, to pull their heavy load toward the river banking grounds.

Each doing his own particular job, the men worked quickly. There was a sort of rhythm in their teamwork.

One day after spending his noon hour with the woodcutters, Corky decided to head south into the heavier untouched part of the section. Here the snow was unmarked by footprints. The trees were not yet touched by ax or saw. The untrampled snow was deeper than Corky had realized, and walking was difficult. When he came upon a footpath through the snow, he gratefully followed it, rather than wade through knee-deep snow.

Shinglebolt, trotting in front of Corky, halted. The hackles over his shoulders and back rose. Corky peered ahead, taking a firmer grip on his rifle. Shinglebolt stepped forward slowly, growling and baring his teeth.

Corky felt the hairs on his neck prickle. It wouldn't be a bear, he reckoned. Bears should all be hibernating in their winter dens.

Shinglebolt crept ahead, slinking low, his furry chest brushing through the deep snow. Corky followed close. With horror Corky saw why the dog growled. A man lay crumpled in the snow. Shinglebolt sniffed the still figure, and his growling changed to whining. The huge dog began licking snow from the man's face.

Corky never had seen a dead person before, yet somehow he knew the man was dead. The eyes were open and unmoving. Still, Corky had to make sure. Tearing off his mittens, he pulled open the man's coat and shirt until he could slip his hand beneath the woolen undershirt. Corky's warm hand pressed against the cold bare chest. No faint heartbeat beneath the icy skin. He held the man's wrist and felt no beating pulse.

With a gulping sob, Corky rose and stumbled back through the woods toward the sound of axes. By the time he reached the tote road and found some shanty boys, he was gasping.

"Help!" he wheezed.

The man known as Big Swede pushed Corky down onto a pine stump. He rubbed Corky's bare hands and said, "Take it easy, lad. Take it easy. Just catch your breath first."

After taking some deep breaths Corky was able to blurt out his horrible discovery. A loud murmur rose from the group of woodsmen gathered around.

Big Swede said, "Can you show us where?"

Corky nodded and started off at a trot.

"Hurry, men," Big Swede motioned the others. "We got to hurry. He could be freezing to death."

Corky, followed by Shinglebolt, led the way.

When they found the body, Big Swede knelt quickly, shouting, "It's Davy McClain!" He examined the still figure, looking for a sign of life, but Corky was right. The man was dead.

The shanty boys grouped around the dead man and stared silently. One of the men gasped in a hoarse whisper, "A Hodag must've got him!" With a lurch, the whole group dashed away, crashing and stumbling through the brush, heading toward the tote road. Only Big Swede, Corky and a tall, older man were left. The two men grunted in disgust at the retreating shanty boys.

The older man spoke first. "Well, let's get him back to camp, Swede. The boss will know what to do."

Big Swede picked up the mittens Corky had dropped when checking the man. "These yourn, sonny?"

Corky nodded, wishing his lips would stop quivering. Big Swede patted his shoulder. "You did a good job, lad. Don't think about those stupid shanty boys. No Hodag killed Davy."

Big Swede pointed to a wound on the back or the dead man's head. "Poor Davy was done in by a cant hook, or a peavey. There's a killer around here somewhere. But it's a two-legged man."

Chapter 9
The Awful News

The camp was in an uproar. The killing of Davy McClain was all the shanty boys talked about. At first some of the shanty boys were going to leave the camp. They refused to work in the territory of a Hodag. Pa, with the help of Big Swede, finally convinced the terrified men that Davy McClain was killed by another woodsman, someone who carried a cant hook or a peavey.

One at a time, Pa questioned all the men, trying to learn if someone in camp had a grudge against Davy McClain. No one knew of any enemy the poor man might have had. He had been a hard worker, he was well-liked, and he owed no one any money.

Charlie built a pine coffin, and the following morning burial services were held in the mess hall. Since there was no preacher, Pa read verses from the Bible, while all the shanty boys shuffled uneasily, staring at the unpainted coffin resting on one of the tables. Davy's peavey lay across the coffin, and it would be buried with him. A dead man's peavey was said to be jinxed, and was never to be used again.

Pa said a brief prayer, and then spoke quietly about what a good man Davy McClain had been. "Cadje has gone to the Big Rapids to summon the sheriff," Pa announced. "Now, we don't know if anyone in this camp is the murderer, or not. I hope and pray it was a stranger passing through our woods. In any case, the sheriff and I will do everything we can to find out who committed this foul killing, so that Davy McClain can be avenged. If any of you remember anything that could help in finding Davy's killer, I want you to tell me or the sheriff when he gets here. You owe that to our friend, Davy McClain. Now, let's all get back to work."

Corky hung around the stable the rest of the morning, helping Frenchie grease harness and trying to get his mind off Davy McClain. He picked listlessly at his noon meal in the cook shack with Gus and Frenchie. Finally, he decided to go into the woods to hunt game for Shinglebolt.

He followed a new trail, carefully avoiding the area where he'd found Davy McClain.

The beauty of the woods lifted his spirits. He sauntered along, watching for rabbit tracks. When a low growl suddenly came from Shinglebolt, a hot flush of fear gripped Corky. The awful memory of finding Davy McClain returned with fresh terror. "Oh, no, not again," he groaned. Corky took a couple deep breaths, feeling ashamed that he was shaking.

Shinglebolt slunk forward, rumbling. Corky wanted to turn and run back the way he'd come, but he remembered the shanty boys running away. He couldn't do that. He had to force himself to take each step to follow the dog.

Shinglebolt stopped still, baring his teeth. Corky saw with horror that there were *two* still figures lying on the snowy ground ahead. Two! He felt his lunch rise in his throat, burning, and he leaned over, retching. When he lifted his head to look again at the two bodies, they both stirred. Shinglebolt snarled. The two figures jumped to their feet, one of them grabbing his ax.

Corky gasped with relief. They weren't dead! Only sleeping.

The man with the ax crouched, ready to swing the ax into Shinglebolt. "Call off your dog, or I'll split him wide open!" he cried.

Corky threw his arms around the dog's neck, trying to pull him back. "It's okay, Shing. Back, Shing, back!" He dug his mittens deep into the dog's heavy fur scruff. Shinglebolt sat back on his haunches and quit baring his teeth, but the rumbling growl continued.

"Don't hurt him, mister!" Corky cried. "He won't hurt you."

"Get out of here!" the man snarled. "And don't let that cur get near me again, or I'll kill him. I seen what he did to that black bear, and I ain't giving him a chance to do it to me. That dog's a killer, and I ain't going to put up with him pestering me! Now git!"

Corky stared up at the menacing ax. He saw that the man had only one ear. A wrinkled scar clung to the head where an ear should have been.

The man's lips curled into an ugly snarl. He yelled, "I said git!"

Corky fled, coaxing Shinglebolt with him, but they had gone nearly half a mile before the dog stopped his protesting growl.

Corky headed straight for the stable. He didn't feel like hunting any more today. Shuffling into the stable, shoulders drooping, he sank down on a grain sack.

Frenchie rubbed his long black moustache and grinned at Corky. "What's the matter, boy? Deer too smart for you today?"

"Naw." Corky kicked at the dirt floor with the heel of his boot. "Just didn't feel like hunting today, I guess."

He decided not to tell anyone about the encounter. Pa might get the idea that Shinglebolt was a mean dog. Dogs weren't supposed to go around growling at people. Corky figured Shinglebolt growled because he remembered Davy McClain lying dead in the snow. Even so, he guessed he'd keep it to himself. He did wonder why those two men were out there alone, sleeping, when they should have been working, and he wondered who they were.

That night during supper in the mess hall Corky slyly peered around until he discovered the two men at the next table. The shanty boys ate greedily with almost no conversation until they began washing down their last wedge of raisin pie with steaming coffee. Then the kidding and joking began. Corky learned that one of the men was called Chicago Pete. The other fellow, the one-eared man who threatened Shinglebolt, was One-Ear Floyd. Corky vowed to keep Shinglebolt far away from them.

That night after climbing into bed, Corky picked up the heavy copy of *David Copperfield* and opened it to the marker where Pa had stopped reading the night before. He and Pa were taking turns reading it every night, and it was Corky's turn. As Corky turned a page, he glanced over at his father and saw that Pa was not listening, but was rubbing his whiskered jaw and frowning. Corky struggled on through another page, but he couldn't concentrate. Pa was worried over something.

"What's the matter, Pa? You aren't listening, and this is a good part."

"I'm sorry, son. Guess I was thinking of something else." Pa sighed as he climbed out of bed to find his tobacco pouch. "I'm worried about what's going to happen when the sheriff gets here."

Corky closed the book and sat up cross-legged on the bed. "Well, the sheriff will find out who killed Davy McClain, won't he?"

"I wish he could," Pa said. "But it's not always that easy to discover a murderer, especially when there aren't any witnesses. We don't even know the reason for the killing."

"You mean we may never know who did it?" Corky leaned forward.

"Perhaps not. But I'm afraid the sheriff may arrest someone on suspicion of murder, and I don't think that person is guilty." Pa finished tamping the tobacco in his pipe and struck a match.

Shivering, Corky pulled the quilt around his shoulders. "Who do you think the sheriff will arrest?"

"I'm afraid it might be poor Elroy," Pa answered.

Poor Elroy, with the twisted face and childlike mind, who had once been normal, before the bank caved off and flung him and his team of horses down the long chute.

Corky spoke quietly. "Elroy *is* kind of strange. I don't like being around him. He scares me."

Pa's eyes flashed anger for a moment, then softened. "That's because you don't know him, son. Don't ever fear someone just because he's different. You haven't been around Elroy enough. Even with his injured head, Elroy is the kindest, most gentle man in this camp. Why, he won't even skin out game, to say nothing about hunting and killing it. After his accident, when he first was able to get up and around, we thought he could help Gus in cutting up deer carcasses and skinning rabbits. Instead, he just held the dead animals, rocking and crooning, with tears running down his cheek."

"I didn't know that," Corky said. "The sheriff won't arrest Elroy if you say he couldn't have done it."

Pa snorted. "I wish it were that easy. The trouble is the shanty boys have been talking among themselves. Many of them have decided that the only possible culprit is Elroy. You say Elroy scares you. The shanty boys have decided Elroy scares them."

Corky blinked. "I'm sorry, Pa. I shouldn't have said that about Elroy."

"You were just admitting what was true, that you were frightened of Elroy. It seems to be a trait of us human beings to be afraid of someone different, of someone we don't understand. I should have guessed that they'd point the finger at Elroy. I almost wish I'd let them go on thinking that Davy got caught by a Hodag."

"But then the men all would have left!" Corky protested.

"Not all of them, but most. I wouldn't have got much timber cut this winter." Pa ruffled his sandy hair. "It's a rotten deal all the way around. I don't know what I can do."

Pa's worries were justified. When Cadje arrived, guiding the sheriff, his deputy and an extra horse into camp, Pa spent several hours talking with them. He showed them the spot where Davy McClain's body was found. The sheriff spent the evening in the bunkhouse talking with the men. The next morning he arrested the bewildered Elroy on suspicion of murder.

Pa protested and pleaded, but the sheriff could not be swayed.

"The accused can't account for his time on the day of the murder," the sheriff said.

"Thunderation, man!" Pa cried, "Elroy can't account for his time any day. He doesn't know time or days. He eats when he's hungry and sleeps when he's tired. He doesn't have a watch or a calendar, and he wouldn't know how to use them if he did!"

The sheriff's mouth tightened. His voice was stern. "So much the worse for him. He's just plain addled, and people like that don't know what they're doing. You're lucky he didn't murder you all in your beds."

Corky blinked back tears when the sheriff and the deputy rode off with Elroy, the poor man's wrists tied to the saddle horn. Until they rode out of sight, Elroy kept looking back, his one eye wide with confusion, his twisted mouth working soundlessly.

Pa said they were taking him to the county seat at the Big Rapids, where there would be a trial.

Two days later Pa told Corky that he was leaving for the Big Rapids to see how Elroy was faring in jail and to find out when his trial would be held. Pa said he was going to hire the best lawyer he could find to defend Elroy against the murder charge. Then he added the awful news.

Chapter 10
The Crack of a Rifle

"Corky," he said, "when I get back, we'll plan to take you back to Muskegon."

"Oh, no, Pa! Not yet!" Corky cried.

Pa insisted. "If you get back soon, you can get in on the spring term. With hard work, perhaps you can make up what you've missed this winter." Pa rested his hand on Corky's shoulder. "I know you want to stay here, son, and I enjoy having you with me. But you must get your school learning."

Corky's shoulders drooped.

"You know I'm right," Pa said softly. "You think about it while I'm gone."

Corky felt depressed when Pa rode off. It was lonely without Pa, not just in Muskegon, but here at camp, too. Corky knew that Pa must go do what he could for Elroy. Even so, he hated having Pa gone. It reminded him of all his lonely winters in Muskegon. As Pa and his dapple gray horse disappeared on the snow-packed trace, gulped up by the dense forest, Cadje invited Corky to join him hunting venison.

"Shanty boys tired of pig meat," he said. "Want deer. We go get fat deer, oui?"

Corky felt too depressed to go hunting. What good was learning how to be a good hunter if Pa was going to send him back to Muskegon? He made an excuse about having to read a book Pa had assigned him as a sort-of school work.

After reading for an hour, Corky grew restless. With Shinglebolt at his heels, Corky sauntered around camp, kicking at frozen clods of snow and brooding over the terrible murder of Davy McClain and the arrest of Elroy. On top of these events, he had his own special worry, something he couldn't talk about with anyone. Pa would scoff at his concern. Cadje and the shanty boys would listen and believe, sharing his uneasiness, but they would get all superstitious and upset.

Because winter was nearing its end, Corky worried about the coming river drive, and The Haunt's sinister warning that Pa should beware of danger at Snowtown Piers. Corky couldn't forget the look in the eyes of The Haunt as he said, "Beware of Snowtown Piers." He might brush off that eerie warning, but he couldn't forget Shinglebolt's strange howling as they passed that bend in the river. Everyone knew that dogs had better senses of hearing and smell than humans. Maybe dogs were smarter in another way. Perhaps they could sense future danger or evil spirits.

Corky pulled a long icicle off the eaves of the cabin and flung it at the rain barrel. "Ugh," he snorted, "Evil spirits!" He was getting as bad as the shanty boys with their Hodag.

Corky forced himself to stop fretting over imaginary dangers. He set about rolling huge balls of snow up against the side of the cabin. After he'd rolled several big snowballs under the roof, he shoveled snow until he had completely filled in an area from the roof to the ground. For the rest of the day he and Shinglebolt had a great time climbing up the snowy slope to the peak of the roof and sliding down to the ground.

On the day Pa was supposed to return, heavy snow began dropping softly in huge moist flakes. Pa wasn't expected until nightfall, and Corky wondered how to pass the day. Cadje had brought back two fat deer carcasses, one of which was a tough old buck, which Cadje said was for Shinglebolt. "Spirit dog have strong teeth. Old buck for spirit dog," said the Indian.

With a whole deer carcass hanging in the shed for Shinglebolt, Corky didn't need to go hunting, but he was restless. He decided to explore the woods for awhile. What if Pa sends me back tomorrow? worried Corky. "This might be our last walk in the woods, Shing," Corky said to the dog.

Shinglebolt tipped his head, trying to understand.

Corky clapped his hand to his mouth. An awful thought had hit him. What would happen to Shinglebolt when Corky was sent to

Muskegon? Aunt Tishia would never let him have a dog. Even sweet Aunt Phoebe wouldn't accept such a huge dog. How could they feed him in Muskegon? He couldn't shoot game for Shinglebolt there.

Corky fell to his knees and hugged the big dog. "Oh, Shing. I can't leave you, but I can't take you." He buried his face in the white furry mane and sobbed.

Finally Corky rose to his feet. "Let's take a walk," he gulped.

It was getting colder. Large snowflakes piled up on the old snow like a thick layer of feathers. Corky fastened on his snowshoes and struck out on the wide path to the banking grounds, where the towering piles of cut logs grew taller each day. He practiced moving his feet in a steady rhythm, toes pointed outward as Cadje had taught him. Not used to snowshoes, he shuffled clumsily. The snow was so deep that even Shinglebolt was tired by the time they reached the banking grounds. There the snow was tramped firm from the heavy teams and sleds pulling logs from the forest. Corky gazed in awe at the huge mountains of logs stacked on the edge of the cliff. These colossal stacks lay poised, waiting only for a push to send them tumbling down the long rollway into the river far below.

For some time Corky and Shinglebolt watched the teams come out of the woods with their burdens of logs. The men added the logs to the huge piles already there, then driver and team returned to the woods for another load.

Corky rose, brushing snow from the shoulders of his overcoat. A strong wind whistled through the pine needles far above. Out over the frozen river, the wind whipped snow so violently that Corky couldn't see across the river.

"Let's go farther down-river, Shing," said Corky. "Gerry's Rocks are down that way somewhere, but I don't know how far." The shanty boys sang a song about the jam on Gerry's Rocks, about Jack Monroe who was killed while breaking the log jam, along with six Canadian boys. Woodsmen said Gerry's Rocks was another name for The Big Bend not far downstream from Pa's camp. It was the first dangerous twist that Pa's river drivers had to face on the spring log drive.

When Corky had come up river in the canoe with Cadje, he had rounded so many bends that he couldn't remember which was which, except for the horrible Snowtown Piers, where Shinglebolt howled the whole way.

Corky and the dog moved down river on the path. After traveling some distance they came to a small clearing surrounded by thick pine forest. The wind whirled through the unprotected clearing, churning snow into a dense cloud.

Corky held his mittened hands over his nose and mouth to breathe warmer air. As he shuffled awkwardly around the edge of the clearing, he discovered a faint, narrow path. It seemed to lead into the woods away from the river. Corky decided to follow it a ways.

He could tell the trace wasn't used much. It was overhung with branches and very narrow, making it difficult to toe out his snowshoes properly. He could feel hard-packed snow beneath the new fluffy snow, so he knew the trail had been trampled hard before today's snowfall.

The path twisted and curled itself into the woods. Corky supposed it was a deer trace. Before long the narrow trail opened into another clearing, larger than the last. With a deep bark, Shinglebolt bounded ahead, plowing belly-deep through the fluffy, blowing snow. His black nose twitched as he snuffed the crisp air.

Corky snowshoed a short distance into the clearing. The frigid wind roaring down into the forest opening soon had him shivering. He whistled for Shinglebolt and turned back toward the narrow trace he had followed, ducking his chin and pulling his coat collar high around his neck. He scarcely could see through the blowing snow as he moved toward the sheltering woods. He slid cautiously through the blinding white blur.

His left snowshoe suddenly struck something solid, and Corky pitched forward onto a snowy mound. As he pushed himself to a standing position, his mittened hands discovered the little hill was actually a pile of logs, frosted with a layer of snow. He brushed the snow off some of the logs and saw that they weren't really logs. They were only six-inch slabs sliced off the end of a log. Peering closer, he saw that Pa's log mark "JB" was branded on one side of each six-inch slice.

Puzzled, Corky whistled again for Shinglebolt. Through the whirling flakes, Shinglebolt bounded toward him. At the same moment he caught sight of the plunging dog, the crack of a rifle sounded nearby. With horror, Corky saw Shinglebolt twist into the air, somersault, and drop to the ground.

Even before he could scream, a smothering blanket fell over Corky. Forceful hands shoved him to the ground. He tried to kick, but the snowshoes were fastened to his boots. There was a heavy thud against the back of his head. Bright lights burst and bounced in his brain. The flashing lights faded, and everything turned black.

Chapter 11
Catch the Murdering Thieves!

No one at Barden's camp slept that night.

Just as the men began their evening meal, Julius Barden rode in from the Big Rapids. Cadje met his boss at the stable.

"What's the trouble, Cadje?" Barden asked.

"Boy and spirit dog not back from woods, boss. Tode Sherman saw 'em at banking grounds mid-afternoon."

Julius Barden's ruddy cheeks blanched to gray. "Lord help us," he whispered, his arms dangling limp. Then, bracing his shoulders, he took charge. "Let the men finish eating. Cadje, round up snowshoes and lanterns. Get all hands out. Everyone head for the banking grounds, and spread out from there." Cadje moved to go, when Barden reached out and touched the Indian's forearm. "He has the dog with him. He'll be all right, won't he, Cadje?"

Cadje gripped his boss's hand warmly. "Spirit dog watch boy," he agreed.

Within the hour, fifty men, some on snowshoes, all carrying kerosene lanterns, moved into the woods to search for Corky and his giant dog. It had stopped snowing, but tracks made in the afternoon were now covered by snow. The boy and dog couldn't be tracked by footprints. The men called and whistled. Swinging lanterns flickered through the forest like summer fireflies.

It was Cadjetan Padou who found Shinglebolt. Cadje entered the clearing by the same path Corky and the dog had taken. He was circling the clearing when he heard a faint whine and quickly turned toward the sound. He spotted the giant dog lying beside a pile of logs, nearly covered with snow. The dog whined again and the bushy white tail gave a feeble shake.

"Boss!" shouted Cadje. "Boss! I find dog! Here!"

His shouts carried far in the frigid air. Soon Julius Barden and three shanty boys came crashing through the brush into the clearing.

Kneeling beside the dog, Cadje examined Shinglebolt. His face contorted sadly as he looked up into his boss's anxious eyes. "Spirit dog shot," he said softly. "Here," he pointed to the upper part of Shinglebolt's right hind leg.

"Where's my son?" cried Barden, moving frantically about through the deep snow. The men spread out through the clearing, shuffling their feet. They kicked every mound of snow in case it might conceal a young boy felled by a bullet.

At last they satisfied themselves that Corky was not in the clearing. "Maybe when the dog was shot, he ran off and got away," Barden mumbled, looking at Cadje for some hope.

One of the shanty boys cleared his throat. "Maybe the boy shot the dog accidentally, and he's afraid to come back to camp."

Julius Barden whirled on the speaker, his fist slamming into the jaw of the surprised man. The man staggered and fell to his knees. Cadje jumped quickly against his boss, shaking him like a naughty child. "No, boss! No!"

Barden came to his senses. He gulped. It was almost a sob. In a trembling voice he said, "I'm sorry, Tom." He reached down and helped the man to his feet.

A shout from one of the men ended the difficult moment. "Here's the lad's Henry, settin' here in the snow!" The shanty boy held up Corky's rifle.

Another man cried, "Look, boss! Someone's been sawing your log mark off and stashing the ends here. See? On every consarned one of 'em," he kicked at several of the log-ends.

The five men exchanged alarmed glances. This probably meant that Corky had stumbled upon the illegal operations of timber rustlers, thieves who stole logs by sawing off the branded end and re-branding the fresh end with their own log mark.

Barden clutched at Cadje frantically. "We've got to find him!" he cried.

Through clenched teeth Cadje muttered, "We find him, boss." The Indian stroked the injured Shinglebolt. "Spirit dog find boy fast."

Barden looked down at the limp, wounded dog. "That dog won't walk for days. He can't help us." His voice was flat.

"You go look, boss," said the Indian. "I work on dog's leg. My medicine strong. By-and-by spirit dog help."

Throughout the long night, the lanterns of Barden and his men flickered and twisted through the woods, while Cadje worked his healing powers on the St. Bernard. Once the bullet was removed and a drawing poultice applied to the wound the dog showed more life, raising his huge head. Before long, he tried to rise, but Cadje pressed the animal down, crooning softly to him, as to a fretting baby. Cadje kept warm poultices on the bullet wound, heating fresh packs on his crackling campfire, keeping pemmican broth simmering over the fire.

When finally the great dog insisted upon sitting up, Cadje removed the skillet from the hot coals, and threw fistfuls of snow into the bubbling broth to cool it.

"*Oui*, this make you better, Spirit Dog," said Cadje as he placed the warm broth beneath the huge muzzle. The Indian watched, satisfied, as Shinglebolt lapped up the entire contents of the frying pan.

As Shinglebolt finished the final drop of broth, he shook his head violently, throwing off the last of his stupor. His muzzle lifted, he cried a mournful howl. Then, holding his injured hind leg high, tucked against his belly, the dog limped off across the clearing in a rocking, three-legged gait. Cadje hastily gathered up his frying pan and kicked snow over the hot coals. He fastened on his snowshoes and hurried after the dog.

The sky above the clearing was growing lighter. Dawn was near.

※   ※   ※

About the same time, as the stars began to fade from the sky, Corky awoke, shivering violently. Through chattering teeth, he moaned, "Shinglebolt!" The last thing he remembered was the awful sight of Shinglebolt somersaulting in the air as a bullet struck him.

With a sob, Corky tried to rise. He struggled for some time before realizing that his hands and feet were bound. His boots were tied together, his wrists anchored behind him.

He struggled to a sitting position and looked around. It was dark, but there was a lighter area which seemed to be an opening. The image of Shinglebolt lying back in the clearing pounded through Corky's head. Finally, anger overcame his fright, quieted his sobs, and brought him strength.

Sitting sideways, Corky tried to bend down to bite the binding ropes of his boots, but he couldn't reach quite that far. He twisted his hands and wrists violently, trying to loosen the binding, but that only made his wrists sore. As he sat there shivering, he wriggled his toes. With a start, Corky realized that his chilled feet were loose in the boots. Concentrating, he worked and pulled until his left foot slipped out of its boot and was free. By using his freed foot, he quickly pulled out the other foot. Now, both his feet were unbound. Corky knelt over the still tied-together boots. Working with his teeth and one elbow, he managed to slip the ropes off. Quickly, he slid his feet back into his boots and rose, limping stiffly toward the daybreak glowing into the cave.

Blinking and shuddering, Corky gazed out of the opening. He was in sort of a dugout on a brush-covered hillside. He tried to figure where he was, but he couldn't tell. Corky struggled to loosen the rope binding his hands behind him, but his shoulders shook so uncontrollably that he nearly collapsed. I'd better just get out of here, he decided. Somehow, he must find the clearing and Shinglebolt. Besides, whoever it was who brought him here might come back, any time. Corky stumbled out onto the snowy hillside and began working his way along the slope. He didn't want to go into the valley at the bottom of the hill. He knew the snow would be deeper there. With his hands tied behind him, walking was difficult. Time after time, he tumbled, head long. Soon he was exhausted since he couldn't use his hands to catch himself or to push himself upright.

He struggled on. Each pound of his heart seemed to pump the word, "Shinglebolt," breaking up any plan that might be forming. After a quarter-hour of stumbling along, Corky sprawled in the snow and was too worn out to get up. As he lay on his side in the cold snow, shivering, he faced the truth. He might be freezing to death. Perhaps he shouldn't have left the shelter of the dugout.

His breath came in gasps with each shiver. Now that he wasn't plowing through deep snow, his mind grew clearer. Maybe I'm not too far from Shinglebolt right now, he reckoned. Whoever got me to the dugout must have carried me. So the dugout must not be too far from the clearing where they caught me, and shot — He shook violently as he relived the crack of the rifle shot and Shinglebolt falling. Wonderful Shinglebolt, with his loving brown eyes and huge white paws.

It seemed he almost could hear the gruff bark of his big shaggy dog. Frowning, he pushed himself with his elbow until he was sitting. He heard it again — Shinglebolt's excited bark.

"Shinglebolt!" Corky yelled. "Shinglebolt! Where are you?"

With a loud crashing of underbrush the white dog emerged on the slope above Corky. A whirlwind of snow rushed downhill as the giant dog churned toward Corky. Shinglebolt nuzzled and licked Corky's shining face as Cadje slid down the hillside in the dog's trail.

※ ※ ※

In less than an hour Corky lay in his own bed in Pa's cabin, enveloped in warm comforters. A flannel-wrapped hot brick warmed his feet. Beside the bed on the floor lay Shinglebolt, a fresh warm poultice covering his leg wound.

Neither warm broth nor heavy blankets could stop Corky's shivering, but he was hardly aware of it. Content that Shinglebolt was safe beside him, Corky drowsed. It was impossible to sleep for long, though, because he felt as if he were floating in the air above the bed, a sensation which made him dizzy. Every so often, someone, he guessed it was Pa, put a cold palm on his hot forehead or pulled the blankets back and put an ear to his heaving chest.

"It's lung fever, Cadje," Julius Barden moaned. "I know it is. He's burning up, and his lungs are rattling. I'm going to get Doc Weatherby. Yesterday I met him on the track to Morley. I think I can catch him there and get him back here by sundown."

Barden gripped the Indian's brown hand. "I wouldn't leave Corky with anybody but you, Cadje. I know you'll do your best by him."

Cadje nodded as he watched his boss scramble into coat and scarf.

Barden would have preferred to stay with Corky himself and send Cadje for the doctor. But he suspected that the busy doctor would be more likely to return at *his* request than at the Indian's.

Cadje sat at the foot of Corky's bed, touching his skin, listening for changes in the strained breathing. Barden hadn't been gone two hours when Corky's breathing became harsher and tighter. Cadje bit his lip.

He could not wait for the white man's doctor. He knew what this sick boy needed.

The Indian summoned Charlie, the bull cook, to stay with Corky. Cadje hurried into the woods beyond the camp buildings toward the small, dome-shaped wigwam which was his sweat lodge. Quickly, he built a fire just outside the blanket-flap door. As the fire grew to its needed intensity, Cadje crawled inside and pushed out the iron tray filled with stones, slid the round stones into the fire, and while they heated, he carefully brushed snow off the rounded dome roof. Next, he broke green boughs off nearby cedar trees, placed them in an iron kettle near the fire, filled the kettle with snow, which the heat of the fire would turn to water.

When Cadje judged the stones to be hot enough, he poked them out of the fire with a forked stick and pushed them onto the flat iron tray which had a rope anchored to one side. The Indian pulled the tray of hot rocks inside the lodge. He crawled back out to get the water-soaked cedar boughs from the kettle. Back inside the lodge, Cadje shook the wet boughs over the rocks. The water hissed against the heated rocks, and great clouds of pungent steam rose in the small round wigwam.

Cadje crawled out of the steam-filled lodge and began building up the fire again. Soon he dragged the tray of rocks out of the lodge and prodded the rocks into the flames to re-heat.

When Cadje was satisfied that the inside of his sweat lodge was steaming warm, he hurried back to the Barden cabin to fetch Corky.

Charlie watched, frowning and blinking, as Cadje wrapped the dozing boy in warm blankets and lifted him from the bed. "You're taking him to your sweat lodge, ain't you, Cadje?" Charlie growled an uncertain disapproval.

Cadje grunted. "Oui. Sweat lodge what boy need. I bring back by and by. You stay with spirit dog. He want to come, but leg need rest."

Cadje carried Corky through the snow-carpeted woods to his misty sweat lodge.

For half an hour Corky lay comatose, aware of nothing. Cadje crawled in and out repeatedly, pushing before him freshly heated rocks and sprinkling them with wet cedar boughs. During this time the only sounds were the rasping wheezes of Corky's labored breathing and the hissing of water on hot stones. At last the steamy air did its job. Corky's breathing grew smooth and quiet.

As his condition improved, Corky's drowsy mind flickered through many hazy memories. He saw Miss Swensen's frowning face float past, and Aunt Tishia's claw-like finger shook at him angrily. He heard the cackling laugh of The Haunt, the crack of a rifle during a snowstorm, and then a growling voice saying, "Not a kid, Floyd! Rubbing out Davy McClain was one thing, but not a kid!"

When Corky awoke back in his own bed, he had only a vague recollection of his strange trip to Cadje's sweat lodge. His fever had broken and his lungs were clearing by the time Pa burst into the cabin with Dr. Weatherby.

The bearded doctor felt Corky's head, counted his pulse rate, and placed an ear on his chest. "The fever has broken. His lung congestion is loose. Are you sure he was as bad as you told me?" he asked.

Pa explained Corky's symptoms only five hours earlier. As he spoke, his eyes narrowed and wandered to Cadje, who stood solemnly in the far corner of the small room.

"When did he start getting better, Cadje?" he asked.

Cadje looked down at his moccasins, then turned his eyes directly at his boss. "He get better after I take him to sweat lodge. I steam *la grippe* out of his chest."

Pa sputtered. "You mean you took that boy out into the cold air, way out to your sweat lodge? Why..."

Dr. Weatherby laid his hand on Barden's forearm. "Hold on, Julius. Many doctors believe that warm, moist air is the treatment of choice in lung congestion. Something broke the fever and loosened the chest inflammation. It might well have been the sweat lodge treatment." He scratched his dark beard thoughtfully. "I'm going to ask around among the local Indians to see if they treat their lung problems this way successfully. It may be that we can learn something from the Indians."

Three days later when Corky had regained some strength, Pa questioned him about the happenings on the night Shinglebolt was shot and Corky tied up in the cave. Corky felt bad that he couldn't identify the culprits. Since he had been hit from behind, he hadn't seen who did it.

"If you think of anything, son, any clues at all, please tell me," Pa pleaded.

"Well, there's one thing," Corky answered. "But it's probably nothing. When I was kind of out of my head in Cadje's sweat lodge, I kept having funny dreams. But they weren't really dreams, just a sort of going over scary things that have happened to me lately. I heard a man's voice saying, 'Not a kid, Floyd! Killing Davy McClain was okay, but not a kid!'"

Pa and Corky talked for a long while, trying to decide if Corky really had heard these words, or whether they were products of a fever dream. They just didn't know.

"I keep thinking of One-Ear Floyd," Pa said. "He's a good river hog, but a mean, despicable cuss."

Then Corky remembered his earlier run-in with One-Ear Floyd and Chicago Pete, where he had stumbled upon them sleeping out in the woods. He told Pa how Shinglebolt had growled at the two shanty boys and how One-Ear Floyd had threatened Shinglebolt with his ax.

Pa questioned Corky carefully about where this took place. Finally, Pa rose. "I'm going to talk with Cadje about this. We'll keep a close eye on those two. They might be murderers. Maybe Davy McClain came upon them, as you did, discovered they were cutting off my log ends, and they did him in. I hate to think I may have murderers on my payroll." He walked toward the door, shaking his head. "I'd sure like to find the real culprits and get Elroy out of jail."

At bedtime, Pa pulled off his heavy boots, then padded across the floor and sat on the edge of Corky's bed. He pressed the palm of his huge hand on Corky's forehead and gently touched the swollen lump on the back of Corky's head.

"I think your fever is nearly gone, son," he said, smiling.

"I feel lots better."

Pa shook his head and grinned. "I think you're going to feel even better when I tell you that I can't take you back to Muskegon for awhile."

Corky sat up abruptly.

"Somebody around here is rustling my branded logs, and that same somebody may be a murderer, to boot. With someone like that around, I don't dare leave to take you to Muskegon, and I need Cadje here, too. Maybe between Cadje and me we can catch the murdering thieves."

"Be careful, Pa," Corky whispered.

"I will. You sleep now and get strong again."

Chapter 12
Gerry's Rocks Ahead!

As the weather warmed, Corky recovered completely. The ground covering of snow grew mushy, and in the daytime, puddles filled every dip and low spot.

One mild morning while Corky was helping grease harness, Frenchie mentioned, "The river's breaking up today."

Corky jumped up. "Wow! I want to see that! Can I go see it?"

Frenchie agreed, and Corky tore off for the river bank.

For the next two days Corky sat on the high bank, fascinated, watching huge cracks split open the thick ice sheet covering the river. The ice had melted away from the shoreline, exposing six feet of open water between the bank and the massive ice sheet. Creaking and crunching, the huge sheet, inch by inch, moved slowly downstream with the current.

The third morning Corky noticed the river level had risen several inches, and the current was rushing faster. At noon the floating sheet made its spectacular break-up. With loud snaps, several large cracks appeared. Then ten-inch thick blocks of ice broke loose from the main sheet and began piling atop each other. More and more dark open water appeared. Floating blocks of ice spun through the open water, slammed into the main sheet, and broke it up further. Groaning and creaking, the whole mass floated downstream with the current, moving faster and faster. By late afternoon the ice sheet was out of sight down river, but huge ice floes still dotted the river, moving swiftly past. For days afterwards huge ice slabs sped by, coming from the break-up farther upstream. The depth and swiftness of the moving water increased daily, rising toward that rapid driving pitch needed to float and speed the logs to the sawmills at Muskegon.

By the first of April the river was free of ice, though several inches of snow still covered the forest floor. This made Pa and all the loggers happy as it was so much easier to skid the huge logs to the banking ground on slippery snow and ice.

The sap in the sugar maples had begun to run, and collecting the sap for the gallons and gallons of maple syrup needed for the hungry loggers was the bull cook's job. One crisp morning just after breakfast Old Charlie found Corky. "I've gotta go out and collect sap buckets this morning, son. Elroy always used to help me, but now that he's amouldering in the Big Rapids jail, I sure would admire your helping me."

At mid-morning Corky and Charlie set out with Oscar, the mule, pulling a huge sled loaded with empty buckets. Shinglebolt padded alongside Oscar, as Charlie led the old mule down the tote road. Corky cradled his Henry rifle in his arm, hoping he might spot a deer for Shinglebolt.

They trudged along easily on the hard-packed snow, talking about who the murderer of Davy McClain might be. Like Pa, Charlie vehemently denied that Elroy could be a killer.

"I disbelieve it," Charlie insisted. "There ain't a mean thought in Elroy's simple head. Why, he won't even go fishing anymore, and me and him used to fish all the time before his dive down the rollway. Now he don't want to hurt the fish."

Corky had a strong feeling, and he knew Pa shared it, that One-Ear Floyd and Chicago Pete were connected with Davy McClain's death. Pa and Cadje had been keeping close watch on those two for several weeks, but as yet had seen nothing suspicious. Once Cadje had trailed them everywhere, unseen, for two days, then reported to Pa in disgust.

"They two lazy shanty boys, boss. They sleep when they suppose to chop. But I see nothing bad, just lazy."

Cadje and Pa frequently checked the clearing where the cut ends of branded logs had been hidden. The clearing remained unused. The guilty party was staying away from there.

Charlie shook his head. "I sure hate to think of Elroy in jail. He's had enough bad luck." He flicked his switch to hurry the plodding mule.

When Charlie and Corky arrived at the section of maple trees which Charlie had tapped, Corky ran up to a bucket hanging from a metal tube sticking out of the tree. It was almost full.

Charlie showed Corky how to remove the full bucket and replace it with an empty one. The bucket containing maple sap was placed in a rack on the sled, where it wouldn't tip and spill. As Corky looked around, he saw they were in a grove of mostly maple trees. As far as he could see through the woods, each maple tree had a dripping tube and bucket.

While they collected and replaced buckets, Shinglebolt wandered, sniffing for a fresh rabbit track. When all the buckets had been exchanged, they headed back to camp with their load of precious maple sap.

As Corky sauntered along beside the cart, his thoughts dwelled on when Pa would be sending him back to Muskegon. With the breakup of the ice and the river rising to log drive pitch, he knew that the time of the river drive was nearing. He tossed a fond glance at Shinglebolt. Whatever would happen to the giant dog when Corky was sent back to Muskegon? Corky blinked as hot tears stung his eyes.

That night Corky could bear the suspense no longer. As they were undressing for bed he asked, "When are you going to send me back to Muskegon, Pa?"

Pa smiled. "Are you ready to go?"

"No," Corky whispered, wishing he'd never asked.

Pa laughed. "Well, if you aren't ready, I guess you can't go, can you?"

The held-in breath rushed out of Corky's lungs in a grateful sigh.

"Actually, I don't have time, son. The river's coming up fast. We'll be breaking the rollways and starting the river drive very soon."

Two days of steady rain broke up what mushy snow remained. The forest floor lay exposed once again. Warm showers and melting snow combined to raise the mighty Muskegon River towards its fullest and swiftest level, what the lumbermen called "driving pitch," that boiling, rushing current which would speed the logs down river with its force. Pa kept a close eye on the ever-rising river.

It had been decided that during the days of the river drive, Corky was to stay on the Wanigan with Charlie. The Wanigan was a rough lumber hut built on a large raft, which would serve as cook shack for the rivermen during the drive. It would float down river behind the log drive, and the food supplies would be stored and cooked in it during the trip.

Just as he did in camp, Gus would do the cooking., He was also in charge of outfitting the Wanigan with the needed foodstuffs. Gus kept Corky and two shanty boys busy hauling supplies down to the Wanigan, which was beached on the shore just below the blacksmith shop.

In preparation for the drive Pa put the spikes on his knee-high boots. Two-inch metal cleats, threaded at one end, screwed into the thick soles of the boots. A flange pierced the sole to keep the spike from slipping. The spikes covered both sole and heel, spaced close, only one-quarter inch apart. When all the spikes were inserted and firm, Pa honed the points sharp. Corky knew that wet logs would be slippery to stand upon without calked boots to bite into the bark.

Corky lifted a boot. "Wow, it's heavy—and big!"

"They're especially large," Pa explained, "because I wear anywhere from three to six pairs of socks with them. That keeps my feet drier and gives me a little cushioning."

On a chilly, overcast morning the river drive began.

Standing on the long plank bench so all the shanty boys could see and hear him, Pa made the announcement at breakfast. "Get your gear stowed on the Wanigan, boys. We've got driving pitch. We'll break Rollway One in a couple hours. Good driving to all of you. We have busy days ahead. I want to see you all safe and sound in Muskegon. Good luck!"

"Good luck!" they howled. "Let's go at 'em!"

"Watch out, Muskegon! Here we come!"

"I can smell Muskegon already! Ain't it sweet?"

Corky wasn't sure if the men were happy because they liked river driving, or if they were excited about heading for Muskegon after a winter's isolation in the woods. He supposed it was the town luring them.

Shanty boys went wild when they got paid in Muskegon at the end of the log drives. With their pockets heavy with a winter's pay, they drank too much and fought recklessly. Aunt Phoebe hadn't allowed Corky out of the house after dark when the shanty boys came in from the drives. "They're like caged wild animals on the loose," she said. "In a few days they'll tame down and be decent again."

Corky arrived at Rollway One long before the others. Off to one side, out of the way, Corky sat on a pine stump and watched the shanty boys gather. Shinglebolt lay down beside the stump, nesting his big head between his paws. The Mackinaw-clad men all wore either red or blue stocking caps. Wide leather belts or bright colored sashes circled their waists. Most of the men wore tobacco pouches dangling from their necks while they carried their matches rolled in the fold of their knit caps. Each man had a pair of mittens tucked into his belt at the middle of his back, out of the way.

Corky wriggled with excitement. Shanty boys who looked like ordinary wood choppers all winter, now showed themselves as colorful, daring adventurers, ready for any perils the river might throw at them.

Corky's job for the duration of the river drive was to be cook's helper. He would have preferred walking along the bank where he could watch Pa and the men maneuvering the logs. But he knew he should work like everyone else. Even so, he disliked being stuck back in the Wanigan at the tail of the drive. He sighed. At least he would be errand boy for Gus. When he helped deliver noon lunch to Pa and the men at the front of the drive, he could see something.

Today Corky didn't have to help Gus until nightfall. Each man had a nosebag lunch tied to his belt. Corky would be free to trot along the high banks, up and down river, watching everything.

His daydreams stopped when he heard the shout, "Knock away the wedges!"

Sledge hammers thumped against the heavy wedges bracing the bottom logs of the high pile, and the wedges fell away. Scarcely breathing, everyone stared at the high mound. Sometimes just releasing the wedges was enough to start the logs down the skidway. There was no creaking or shifting of the stacked logs.

Big Swede, brandishing his peavey, approached the mountain of logs poised on the high cliff and studied how to break the rollway. He clambered over some of the lower logs, squinting as he studied their balance. The big man grunted as he prodded and pushed at the logs. Ice, wedged in crevices, still glued many logs together.

A steady murmur arose from the shanty boys. Some pointed and called advice, each having his own idea of which was the key log, that certain log, which, when moved, would start the whole pile on its downward plunge. Big Swede ignored all suggestions. Breaking the rollway was *his* responsibility. It was *his* life that was endangered if he made the wrong decision.

Swede continued prodding different logs until he hooked his peavey around one log and twisted it to a new angle. There was a rumble like nearby thunder. Swede leaped to one side and safety. The top of the log mountain sank. The bottom logs mushed out, tumbling and skidding helter skelter down the scarred cliff. Beneath Corky's boots the earth trembled as the logs slid and somersaulted end-over-end, thudding against the steep wall of the slope.

The river boiled high, its water displaced by tons of pine logs filling its bed, forcing the water higher and higher on the banks. Tail-end logs were still sliding down the rollway when the shanty boys swarmed down the embankment to the turbulent water. Bright colored hats and sashes bobbed over the river as the men balanced on floating logs. Laggard logs they attacked with their peaveys, shoving them onward, spacing the logs to avoid a dense mass.

"Spread 'em out!" the call echoed across the water.

As the logs slid downstream with the swift current, dark water scarcely showed between the hundreds of logs. Corky watched, fascinated, as the shanty boys danced gracefully over the logs, first poised on one, then hopping to another. He spotted Pa at the far bank of the river. Pa was easy to distinguish from the other men because of his crazy hat with the green crown.

Big Swede moved on to Rollway Two, the next log mountain to be skidded into the river. With the logs from the first rollway moving easily downstream, the second rollway would be broken, the logs floating behind the advance mass. All in all, there were eight rollways located on three different banking grounds.

Corky watched the first four rollways plunge to the water. Then he decided to move downstream to see how the head of the drive was progressing. With Shinglebolt trotting behind, Corky walked nearly an hour before he caught up with the steadily moving logs. He found his father on the river's edge, poling logs out of a small eddy.

"Hi, son," Pa greeted him. "What do you think of it all?"

"I never thought there were so many logs in the whole world," said Corky.

Pa nodded. "It's a bunch. And just think, these are logs from just our operation. Soon we'll be running into logs from other camps. Already we're pushing a few laggards from Buck Benedict's camp. We met a timber cruiser a ways back, and he says the river is full between Newaygo and Croton. He also said he saw Edward Shilling at Muskegon Forks."

"Who's that?"

"Oh, the man the shanty boys call 'The Haunt.'"

"What's he doing there?"

"I suppose he's getting supplies. I *am* surprised, though. He doesn't usually get out into the world like that."

"Where's Muskegon Forks?"

Pa grunted as he shoved a log back into the current. "About twelve miles downstream, where the Little Muskegon joins the Big Muskegon."

A burly river hog balanced on a high-floating cork pine log swept toward them. He raised his peavey in a salute as the current sped him past. "Ho, boss!" he called. "Gerry's Rocks coming up ahead."

Pa called, "Right, Joe! You stop there and I'll send others down to help you." Pa hailed two shanty boys on the far side of the river. "Get on down to the Big Bend now, men," he called. "Joe will need some help there."

With their peaveys the men each snagged a passing log and jumped aboard, gliding swiftly downstream.

Corky swallowed, feeling his muscles tense. He dreaded this first dangerous river bend.

Chapter 13
"The Haunt" No Longer

Corky stood at the Big Bend of the river, where he could see a good way both up and downstream. Logs had been sliding through for some time. As yet there had been no trouble. On the opposite bank from Corky three shanty boys poled hesitant logs through the wavy riffles near that shore. Below the riffles and more midstream the dangerous "white water" churned and boiled as it broke over Gerry's Rocks. So far, every log had tumbled easily through the rapids. If a log should get snagged and hung up in the rapids, there would be a real problem. The rocks were too far midstream to be reached by a man on shore.

Corky sat down on the cushion of fallen pine needles and absently scratched Shinglebolt's ear. He wondered what The Haunt was doing at the Muskegon Forks. Could the strange man be coming to meet the drive? he wondered. Corky remembered the old man's outburst over the danger to Pa at Snowtown Piers. Perhaps he was coming to deliver his warning again, the warning that Pa should avoid Snowtown Piers.

A shout from the river bank just below Corky brought him to his feet. With a shrill yip, Shinglebolt bounded to the river's edge.

Corky saw the problem. A huge log was hung up in the rocks, crosswise to the rushing current. Speeding logs thudded against the crosswise log, were deflected, and spun onward. But it was just a matter of time. Soon a log would catch there, then another, and a log jam would be born.

Pa's familiar figure joined the shouting and cursing men at the river bank. Corky's mouth grew dry as he saw his father step into the water. With a twist of his torso, Pa leaped onto a passing log which was rushing directly toward the barrier log. Two jumps brought him to the forward end of his mount. He crouched, waiting. In the second before his speeding log slammed into the barrier, he hopped onto the hung-up log. Pa teetered and swayed, but regained his balance with the aid of his peavey.

Corky bit his fist in terror. Dozens of logs were sweeping down on Pa's precarious island.

Pa jammed his peavey against a rock and shoved. For a moment the hung-up log seemed wedged tight. As he leaned his whole weight against his peavey, the log inched sideways. The powerful white water sucked at the loosened log. Suddenly it was free and racing with the current through the rapids, bucking and rocking. Pa's body gyrated violently as he tried to keep his balance on the tumbling log. He managed to stay with the log a few moments, until it bounced against an underwater rock. Pa pitched forward into the rapids.

Corky screamed as Pa disappeared into the boiling white water filled with bone-shattering rocks. Farther downstream a figure darted from the river bank and splashed into the churning water.

"It's Cadje!" Corky gasped.

The Indian thrashed and floated, keeping his eye on one spot. Pa had not rolled and tumbled more than ten yards when Cadje grasped his boss's arm. Pulling and heaving, Cadje turned toward shore. A shanty boy ran along the bank, keeping abreast of the floating men. Cadje splashed and twisted, angling closer to shore. The shanty boy tensed, waiting for the exact moment, then waded into the stream. He thrust his peavey out, and with his free hand, Cadje caught hold. Quickly, the two men were pulled ashore.

Pa lay crumpled and unmoving. Corky chewed on his knuckles, his heart pounding.

Cadje rolled Pa over to lie face down, then began pushing on Pa's back just above his waist. More shanty boys ran up, grouping around their boss. "No, no," Corky mumbled, feeling his eyes sting with tears. He could hardly see.

Then suddenly Pa was sitting up, coughing. He was shaking hands with Cadje, nodding and laughing with the shanty boys.

Corky's knees wobbled as he hurried down the embankment toward Shinglebolt who stood rooted, ears up, alert, not far from the crowd around Pa. Apparently Shinglebolt had watched the whole terrifying episode, and even yet kept staring intently first at the boiling river and then at Cadje and Pa.

"It's all right, Shinglebolt. Cadje saved Pa. Everything's fine. Come here."

Reluctantly, Shinglebolt padded to Corky's side and sat on his haunches, his drooping brown eyes glued to the men gathered around Pa. It seemed to Corky that Shinglebolt was trying to think, studying out what had happened. When Corky's knees stopped trembling he started walking toward Pa.

Pa had suffered no serious injury, though most of his body was bruised. Skin had been scraped from his nose, and one eye was swelling shut. The men convinced him that if he would lie down and rest, he might be fit for work tomorrow. Cadje built a small wigwam from willow saplings and covered it with pine boughs.

Corky watched protectively for more than two hours while Pa slept inside the little round-domed hut. Charlie delivered a small pot of pigeon broth.

"When Gus heard about the boss getting banged around, he had me shoot two pigeons. Gus says this will mend your Pa fast." Charlie shuffled his boots uneasily and left.

Corky built a small fire to keep the iron kettle containing the broth hot. Later, when Pa awakened, he agreed to sip Gus's soup, though he refused to let Corky spoon it to him. "Tarnation, boy!" he grumbled. "I'm not sick — just sore!"

After finishing the broth Pa reclined on one elbow and regarded Corky thoughtfully. "Come in here with me, son," he said. "There's something that's been bothering me, something I should have told you before, and I'm ashamed that I haven't."

Puzzled, Corky crawled inside the wigwam.

"It's about the old man they call 'The Haunt,'" Pa began. "Have you ever wondered about him?"

"I sure have."

"What have you wondered about?" Pa prodded.

Corky cleared his throat. "How come The Haunt knew Mama?"

"What did the old man say to make you think he knew Mama?"

Corky feared he'd pushed the subject too far, but he stumbled on. "He told me what Mama said when she was dying."

A big sigh came from Pa's bed. "Oh, that. Well, the old man was addled by the same fever that killed your mama. I wouldn't put any stock into what he thought he heard her say. He just was having fever dreams."

"You mean he made up the story of Snowtown Piers, and how it takes a logger's life every year for a toll?" Corky asked.

"No," said Pa. "He didn't make it up. Shanty boys have been spreading that legend for years. He just took it to heart a little more than other people."

Now that Pa had brought it up, Corky wanted to pursue the mystery. "But how come he was with Mama when she died? I thought she died in Muskegon."

Before answering, Pa gave a long sigh. "I should have told you about him before this, son," he began. "I really don't know why I didn't, except that Edward is hard to explain.

"That strange old man who everyone calls 'The Haunt' is really Edward Shilling, who was a brilliant university professor for years. Edward met and married a lovely Indian woman. Their daughter was your mother."

Corky's eyes widened.

Pa cleared his throat and went on. "As you know, I brought your mother to Muskegon with me after we were married, and you were born there. Back East Edward's wife died, and the summer you were four years old, Edward came out to visit us. He especially wanted to see you, his only grandchild. While he was staying with us he contracted a serious illness which was going about. Your mother nursed him and brought him out of danger, but in doing so, she caught the fever, and it killed her. The old man was never the same after that. I don't know if it was the grief over your mother's death, or his feeling of guilt because she caught the fever from him. Maybe the high fever addled his mind. Anyway, he was incapable of returning to his professorship. He just wanted to be alone.

"He took to the woods to heal himself and to think, he said. He grew to prefer the wilderness. He insists upon living at that solitary place where you visited him. I suppose he's happy in his own way. He chooses to be off by himself, yet he enjoys company from time to time. I imagine he was excited over seeing you. He's often asked me to bring you up river for a visit."

Corky wrinkled his nose. "You mean The Haunt is *my* grandfather?"

"Well, I wouldn't call him 'The Haunt' if I were you. That's just a name the superstitious shanty boys gave him. They're afraid of anything they don't understand. But since you understand about him, you needn't be afraid of him anymore. He's really a nice old fellow, and still quite brilliant. You can learn a lot just from talking with him. He's traveled, studied abroad, read hundreds of books. And now in his old age, he's an expert woodsman and authority on the ways of the Indians. There isn't much the old gentleman doesn't know. You can be proud to be his grandson."

Corky thought about it. He supposed the old man *was* kind of interesting. "You know, Pa, it was The Haun.." Corky stopped, confused. "What should I call him?"

"I think he'd be delighted if you'd call him 'Grandfather.'"

Corky nodded. "Anyway, I was going to say that it was Grandfather who saved Shinglebolt's life. Cadje was going to stab Shinglebolt because he thought it was a Hodag attacking me. The old man saw right away that Shinglebolt was a St. Bernard trying to save my life. That was real smart."

Corky reached out of the wigwam to scratch Shinglebolt's soft ears.

Pa chuckled and yawned. "Listen, son, I'm going to rest here and heal up. You go back to the Wanigan and stay there with Gus tonight. I'll see you tomorrow."

"Sure, Pa." Corky crawled out of the wigwam. He turned and leaned inside the small doorway. "Take care of yourself, Pa."

Still feeling shaky from Pa's close call, Corky started trudging upstream toward the tail of the drive. His steps got slower and slower until he finally sat down to think.

Pa nearly was killed today, Corky told himself. And there's still Snowtown Piers ahead. If The Haunt, I mean, Grandfather, were here, maybe the two of us together could persuade Pa that he shouldn't be riverhogging. *Grandfather and I*, he thought; *yes, Grandfather and I at least could try.*

Swiftly, Corky turned back downstream, heading into the woods where he wouldn't be seen from the river. He came upon a trail which seemed to be heading more or less downstream and followed that. When he felt positive he was far past the head of the drive, Corky turned toward the river. He would follow the river bank to Muskegon Forks.

Shinglebolt sauntered along easily, sometimes loping ahead, sometimes following. Corky moved at a good pace. He wanted to get to the Forks before dark. With Shinglebolt as his companion, the woods wouldn't be especially frightening, but he wanted to find his grandfather yet this evening. He must get back to the river drive by morning before he was missed.

Throughout the afternoon he was surrounded by early blooming wildflowers and songs of newly returned birds, but he didn't notice. His mind had fastened upon one thing—The Haunt, his peculiar grandfather. The more Corky thought about Pa's narrow escape today, and the dangers lying ahead on the river, the more sure he became that his grandfather was needed.

The more often he said to himself the word "grandfather," the nicer it sounded. It would be good to have a grandfather. He didn't have a mother, but he could have a real grandfather. Why, probably he could learn lots of things from the old man.

Learn. He could *learn*. Right then, the really great idea hit Corky. He stopped walking. "That's it!" he said aloud.

Then, to share his wonderful idea, he turned to Shinglebolt. "Grandfather used to be a teacher. He can be *my* teacher! He can come live with Pa and me at the lumber camp and be my teacher. Then I won't have to stay in Muskegon to go to school. I can be with Pa and you and go to school at the same time!" Shinglebolt nudged Corky's hand for a pat.

Corky walked on, even faster, with a spirited bounce to his steps.

Chapter 14
Snowtown Piers Threatens

The western sky was glowing pink when Corky entered the small settlement of Croton at the forks of the Muskegon River. The first person he met looked like a shanty boy.

"Excuse me, sir," Corky said. "I'm looking for an old man, and I wondered if you had seen him."

The man gaped at Shinglebolt.

Shinglebolt flopped down on the ground and began to roll, scratching his back fur.

"What *is* that?" the man asked, staring open-mouthed at the giant dog.

"He's a St. Bernard," answered Corky. Then he added, "a dog. I'm looking for..."

"I never seen a dog that big," the man said, rubbing his stubbly chin. "He's really a dog, huh?"

"Yes, sir." Corky repeated patiently, "I'm looking for an old man."

"Lots of old men around here, sonny." The man never took his eyes from Shinglebolt, who rose and shook himself, scattering dust. "What does your old man look like?"

"He's my grandfather, and he doesn't live here. He lives down river this side of Old Woman's Bend. I hear he's in town for supplies. He has a long gray beard and he wears deerskin clothes."

The shanty boy turned to Corky, eyeing him curiously.

Corky swallowed and went on. "Some people call him, 'The Haunt.'"

The man laughed. "Why didn't you say so? Everyone knows who The Haunt is. He's up ahead with that bunch of people there, see?" He pointed toward the river bank. "Says he's fishing for turtle." The man snickered.

Corky thanked him and started on.

"Say, sonny," the shanty boy stopped him. "Is that old coot really your grampaw?"

"Yes. Why?"

The man giggled again, rolled his eyes upward, and walked off.

As Corky approached the small group of people standing around The Haunt, he saw that they were laughing and nudging each other, pointing at the small, deerskin-clad figure squatting on the river bank.

Corky's lips pressed together hard. Who do they think they are, making fun of a man like Grandfather? Corky's cheeks burned. Why, I bet Grandfather knows more than all of them put together. And not just book-learning, either. He knows more about the woods and living outdoors, and surviving, and just everything.

Corky pushed his way through the group. Grandfather was clutching a fishing pole made from a branch. He stared intently at the water, oblivious to the commotion around him. Corky touched his bony shoulder. "Grandfather," he said, "it's me. Corky Barden."

The gnarled, bearded face turned swiftly to Corky. He jumped up quickly. There was nothing old about his movements, Corky noticed.

"Wonderful to see you, my boy," Grandfather's reedy voice shook slightly. "Where's your father?" He looked around, beyond Corky. "I see your giant lifesaving friend."

"Pa's not with me, sir. Just Shinglebolt."

"Well, then, what are you doing here at the Muskegon Forks?"

"I came looking for you, sir."

The bushy eyebrows flew up. "Is something the matter with your father?" he asked, squeezing Corky's shoulder.

"No, he's all right," Corky reassured him. Corky glanced around at the staring people. The group stared at Shinglebolt, then at his grandfather. "Can I talk with you alone, Grandfather?"

Grandfather bowed graciously to the crowd. "Excuse us, please," he said elaborately. Taking Corky by the elbow, he led him away from the crowd.

As well as he could, Corky explained about Pa's close call and admitted his worries about Pa's safety on the river drive. "I thought maybe if you would come back to the drive with me, Grandfather, maybe the two of us could get Pa not to do the riverhogging."

Grandfather looked intently into Corky's dark eyes. "Strange, lad. Strange it is. I was on my way to meet your river drive. I didn't think the drive would have started yet." He paused, thinking. "It was at the Big Bend at noon, you say?" He clutched Corky's arm. "We must hurry then to get back there."

Corky discovered walking at night was difficult. Where the trail followed close to the river, the faint moonlight helped. When the trace angled into dense woods, no moonbeams could filter through. During these blind stretches in nearly total darkness, Shinglebolt helped by trotting ahead. Corky could make out the dog's white shape and follow that. Still, time after time, he bumped into trees and tripped.

During the easier stretches, when they could see where they were walking, Corky and his grandfather talked. Corky related the events of the past winter. He told of the murder of Davy McClain and the suspicions about One-Ear Floyd and Chicago Pete, and the sad arrest of Elroy. After a few hours his grandfather didn't seem strange at all. Corky felt as if he'd known his grandfather always.

Some time toward midnight Grandfather insisted they stop and rest. He pulled a strip of deer jerky and a slab of cornbread from a pocket. They sat at the river's edge, chewing the tough, salty meat. When they had finished, Grandfather lit his pipe. Corky sniffed the familiar aroma, the same brand that Pa smoked. It was interesting that both his father and grandfather smoked the same kind of tobacco. Then it occurred to him that Pa undoubtedly supplied Grandfather with the tobacco.

The companionship gave Corky courage to speak of his idea. Grandfather listened silently, puffing, while Corky proposed that he join the household of Julius and Corky Barden and become the teacher of a school with one pupil—Corky.

When Corky finished his proposition, Grandfather cleared his throat. "Most interesting idea. Tutorial learning in a one-to-one relationship between teacher and pupil is the speediest method of education. Is this *your* proposal or your father's?"

Corky gulped. "Mine, sir, I haven't talked with Pa about it yet."

Grandfather made a sound. Corky couldn't tell whether he was chuckling or coughing.

They moved on, following the path as best they could. It was still dark when up ahead from near the river's edge came the sound of voices. Shinglebolt growled. Corky reached out toward the big dog. The hair along Shinglebolt's back was standing straight upright.

The St. Bernard began moving ahead stealthily, his broad chest nearly sweeping the ground. Grandfather and Corky followed cautiously. Corky was bringing up the rear when his boots were snared by a tangled mass of berry bushes. He sprawled forward onto his stomach. As he pulled his legs from the entangling thorns, he heard a shout.

A gruff voice yelled, "You get the dog! I'll take the old man!"

Crouching, Corky cocked his Henry and moved forward. Suddenly, he was face-to-face with One-Ear Floyd and Chicago Pete, each brandishing a cant hook and advancing upon Shinglebolt and Grandfather.

Corky raised the gun and sighted in Chicago Pete. "Stop!" he cried. "Stop or I'll shoot you!"

The two men stopped, their mouths hanging loose. Grandfather leaped to Corky's side.

"Drop those cant hooks right now or you're dead men!" Grandfather's voice rasped.

Chicago Pete dropped his long cant hook immediately, but One-Ear Floyd squinted and studied the boy with a gun. Corky quickly aimed the gun at Floyd's broad chest. With a growl, the one-eared shanty boy dropped his weapon.

"Come here, Shing," Corky called, but Shinglebolt, hackles up, stood his ground, tense and watchful.

"Let him be," Grandfather whispered to Corky.

Along the river bank were many cut slabs of logs bearing the JB log brand. The blade of a two-man saw glinted in the pale moonlight, making it evident what the two men were doing. Corky and his grandfather had caught Chicago Pete and One-Ear Floyd in the act of cutting off the ends of logs bearing the log-mark of Julius Barden. Corky's mind flashed to the clearing where Shinglebolt and he had stumbled upon the pile of cut slabs. That was where Shing was shot, and ...that was it! It *had* been One-Ear Floyd and Chicago Pete who...

Grandfather's thoughts had raced ahead of Corky's. The older man's lips tightened. "You were going to send me the way of Davy McClain, weren't you?" He glared at the two men. "I ought to shoot you both right here and save the judge some trouble. Let me have the gun, lad," he ordered.

Corky's dark head jerked up. "Don't shoot them, Grandfather! Pa wouldn't want that!"

Grandfather shook his head. "I'm not going to shoot them if they behave and keep very still. I'm just going to hold this gun on them while you go get help. We want someone else to see this, and we aren't going to take any chances with these two devils."

Reluctantly, Corky handed his grandfather the Henry rifle. He started off upstream to look for some of his father's shanty boys. When Shinglebolt saw Corky leaving, he whined and pranced restlessly.

Corky called sharply, "Stay! Shinglebolt, stay!"

Though the dog wanted to go with Corky, he accepted the order and stood his ground to help keep the dangerous men at bay.

The first pale hint of dawn was lightening the sky when Corky came upon the first group of Barden shanty boys. While Corky breathlessly told about the dangerous Floyd and Pete, eight men followed him back to where Grandfather and Shinglebolt were holding them captive. At first, Pete and Floyd denied everything about Davy McClain's death.

With a grunt of disgust, a slender blond shanty boy called "Tode" pulled out his pocket knife and faced Chicago Pete. Slowly, the man lifted the knife toward Pete's head. With a jerk Tode grabbed Pete's ear and pressed the knife blade against the top of the ear.

Pete grimaced. "I didn't kill him!" he howled.

"You're a liar," the blond man said quietly. "And I cut the ears off of liars. Your friend here just has one ear, but he's gonna have one more ear than you do." He paused. "Unless you decide to quit lying."

It was very quiet. Pete rolled his eyes innocently. The shanty boy pulled Pete's ear outward and pressed on the blade. A trickle of blood streamed down Pete's temple and he howled, "Don't! Stop! I'll tell you!"

It wasn't a legal way to get a confession. Still, Corky was grateful to the knife-wielding Tode for pulling the truth from the two men.

When Chicago Pete and One-Ear Floyd were escorted back to the river drive, tempers erupted. Everyone was outraged that two shanty boys had murdered another shanty boy.

Some of the men wanted to hang them on the spot.

"Let's have a necktie party!"

"Yeah, a session of Judge Lynch's court, and string 'em up to that hemlock tree!"

Pa convinced the shanty boys that in order for Elroy to be freed of the murder charge, they must deliver the real culprits to the sheriff. He asked for volunteers to help escort the captives to the Big Rapids. Everyone wanted to go. After months in the isolated woods, even a fast trip to the Big Rapids sounded like heaven to the shanty boys. Pa chose four of the hardest workers as a reward for their industriousness. He also asked Grandfather to accompany them since he was an eyewitness. Grandfather could testify against Pete and Floyd, who had attempted to kill him just as they had succeeded in killing Davy McClain.

Two days later just as the men were gathering for their evening meal Grandfather and the four shanty boys returned. Everyone broke into cheers when they caught sight of Elroy, a happy grin on his twisted face.

"Elroy! Ho! Welcome back, Elroy!" The men whistled, clapped and stomped. Joyful tears rolled down Elroy's cheek as the men hugged him and patted him on the back. His crooked mouth twisted and worked as he mumbled happily over and over, "Home. Home."

Corky looked up at Pa and saw that his father's eyes were wet with happiness, too.

It was good to have Elroy back and the real murderers of Davy McClain in jail, but as with many things, there was some bad in it. One-Ear Floyd and Chicago Pete had been Pa's topnotch river hogs. Now they were imprisoned in the Big Rapids jail. This meant Pa and Cadje would have to work all the time as river hogs.

"Well, we've done it before, haven't we, Cadje?" Pa smiled, thumping Cadje on the back.

"Sure, boss. We do it." Cadje made a sour grimace.

Pa laughed. "Yeah, I know your trouble, Cadje. You just hate to put on those calked boots instead of your infernal moccasins."

Cadje nodded and chuckled. "Oui, boss. I not like to wear prickly horseshoes."

Pa and Cadje didn't seem to mind the prospect of being river hogs, but the thought of it filled Corky with uneasiness. Already Pa had survived one close call. Riverhogging was dangerous work, and that old warning rang through his head. He just couldn't forget about Snowtown Piers and the life that dangerous river bend claimed every year.

The speed of the current was slowing. There had been no rain for five days and the snow runoff had gone downstream. Logs slid steadily, in no great hurry to meet their fate at the sawmill.

Between running errands for Gus, and hunting deer for Shinglebolt, Corky had little time to watch the advance section of the drive. When he did see Pa or Cadje, they were too busy to talk. Grandfather had volunteered to keep Gus's wood burning cook stove supplied with kindling. He was often off in the woods, searching out the favored hickory or oak woods, which made the hottest, steadiest fires. Grandfather and Gus had struck up an instant working relationship. The cook seemed to enjoy Grandfather's company.

"You like my grandfather, don't you?" Corky asked Gus. "I do, too. But at first I was afraid of him."

The cook wiped doughy hands on his flour sack apron. "Nothing to be afeared of in him, boy," he said.

"I know," Corky agreed. "But when I first met him he seemed so strange. I didn't like his being different."

Gus thrust both fists into the huge ball of dough he was kneading. "Once, when I ran out of wheat flour, I made flour by pounding cat-tail roots. Cadje told me about doing that. I made biscuits from it, and they was real good. But the shanty boys wouldn't eat 'em. Threw 'em on the floor and stomped 'em. Said they was no good. They was different. Some people is like that, they just don't like nothing *different*."

Corky remembered that at first he'd been afraid of Shinglebolt—afraid of that great gentle dog because of his huge size. He thought of all the mean taunts that Freddie Stone and Maribell Stearn had hurled at him about being part Indian. He remembered that his own mother had been despised. Despised for being *different*, he thought. So many cruelties and misunderstandings go on in the world, just because people won't accept someone being different from them! To think that he'd almost missed getting to know his grandfather, just because the old man was unusual.

I won't be afraid of anyone or anything strange, Corky vowed silently. *I won't fear things I don't know about.* But then he thought of Snowtown Piers, and a cold shiver rippled up his back.

Chapter 15
Spirit Dog or Dog of Spirit

Everyone grew jittery as the parade of logs approached the narrow tight bend of Snowtown Piers. The singing and good-natured joking of the shanty boys ceased. Cadje clumped around angrily in his hated calked boots. Twice Gus shooed Corky from the Wanigan, saying, "Leave a man have some peace and quiet!"

Grandfather spent all his time now trailing and pestering Pa, trying to persuade him to ride the Wanigan through Snowtown Piers. Pa bore the nagging for a time, but then his lips tightened, and he cried, "Get away, Edward! Let it be! It's hard enough for me to handle the silly notions of the shanty boys. I can't be badgered by a superstitious old man!"

Shoulders drooping, Grandfather walked into the woods out of sight.

Pa turned back to the river, bawling orders to the river drivers. "I want five men down on the bend on this bank and three men on the other side. Step lively now, and get down there!"

Cadje drifted along on a log, and Pa called to him, "You take this side, Cadje. I'll get over there."

"Oui, boss," Cadje answered. Pa hopped a passing log, leaped to a nearby log, and then to another, working his way across the river, using floating logs for stepping stones.

Corky trudged down river, approaching warily the dreaded place. When he reached the hated curve, he climbed the steep embankment and leaned against a hemlock, its drooping branches nearly hiding him.

Cautiously he surveyed the looping river. *So this was Snowtown Piers! It didn't look any worse than other river bends*, he thought, relieved. Logs were skimming around the curve easily, with only an occasional prod from a river man on shore.

Corky watched for some time, slowly becoming aware that something was wrong. He felt a vague, creeping sensation of something amiss, but he couldn't tell what it was. He sniffed and listened. Glancing around, he suddenly knew. Shinglebolt was gone. Corky whistled and called, listening for the welcome cracking of brush. But there was no sound. Corky tried to remember when he last saw Shinglebolt. Up river aways, he decided. Shinglebolt never followed me to Snowtown Piers!

Frowning, more puzzled than alarmed, Corky headed back upstream. It was strange, though. Shinglebolt never had strayed from him before. Even so, he supposed he'd find him worrying a raccoon or muskrat somewhere along the bank.

He was puzzling over Shinglebolt's disappearance so intently that at first he didn't hear the shouts and yells. Hands in pockets, he sauntered on up river. With surprise, he nearly collided with Big Swede and two shanty boys, racing down river, hollering, "Jam ahead! Jam ahead!"

Aghast, Corky stared at the disappearing back of Big Swede. A log jam at Snowtown Piers!

Whirling, Corky raced downstream toward the dreaded bend of Snowtown Piers. The booming thunder of colliding logs now met his ears. When Corky reached the sharp curve, he stared in horror at the mass of logs, crashing one atop another, in a hopeless jumbled mess. He noticed with surprise that no one was doing anything. Pa stood on the opposite bank, leaning casually on his peavey.

Corky found Big Swede and asked, "Why isn't anybody trying to break the jam?"

The hefty shanty boy explained that there was nothing they could do yet. Now that the jam had formed, they had to wait for a dense pile of logs to build up. Once the jam became thick enough, it would act like a dam, obstructing the river. The water behind the jam would rise higher and higher, and put tremendous pressure on the jam. Then they would begin to loosen logs to break the jam.

Hundreds of logs careened into the crazy mess, until the leading edge of the logs towered three times the height of a man. Slowly, the river upstream began to rise. Below the jam the river became a mere trickle. Muddy flats were exposed on both sides of the narrowed stream. As logs continued to amass, the river drive, which had been spread out over two miles of river, was now compressed into a monstrous jumble of logs filling not over one-half mile of the river.

"The pressure is gettin' pretty strong, now," said Big Swede, pointing to the high water behind the jam. Every minute the steady current kept adding to the rising river level. He nodded to the opposite river bank. "They'll open up an area between the jam and the shore so's it can't bind on the bank. Then she'll begin to loosen up, and purty soon it'll haul out."

Corky saw a dozen men, including Pa, begin prying and pulling logs from the mountain of logs blocking the river. Corky moved farther downstream so he could see better. With dismay, he gazed at the towering jumble, a cliff poised ready to topple and crush everyone below it.

Slowly, one at a time, logs were cleared, opening a narrow indentation into the huge creaking pile. Twice, when the log mass shuddered and moaned, shanty boys leaped swiftly out of the way, but it didn't break up.

The men returned to their prodding and pulling, finally opening a narrow channel between the shore and the jam. Water boiled through the opening. Bracing themselves against the rushing water, men stood waist-deep, prodding and searching for the key log. Just as Pa twisted loose a bottom log, a deep rumble echoed through the river valley. The lower logs slid out from beneath the tall log mass. The topmost logs tumbled end over end. The jam had hauled.

Everything happened in a blur of speed. Huge logs snapped in half like flimsy matchsticks. With a deafening roar the whole mountain of logs slid like an avalanche. With horror, Corky saw a hurtling log catch his father's leg and topple him into the seething confusion of water and wild logs. A sob broke from Corky's chest. Frantically he searched for Pa's head. There was nothing but tumbling logs. A white blur flashed down the river bank and whirled into the mass of logs.

It was Shinglebolt!

The big dog hit the water, disappeared beneath the surface, then bobbed up. In his teeth he gripped Pa's arm. Thrashing, Shinglebolt swung Pa near shore, where two shanty boys grabbed their boss and pulled him up on the bank, out of the way of the crushing logs.

Sputtering and coughing, Pa stood up, shouting, "Keep those logs moving! Get 'em spread out!"

"He's all right!" sighed Corky. Pa's all right! Shinglebolt saved him!

Corky scanned the opposite shore, expecting to see Shinglebolt climbing ashore. There was only a boiling cauldron of tossing logs. Oh, no! No! Corky choked. Shinglebolt! Where are you?

A firm hand gripped Corky's shoulder. It was Cadje.

"Spirit dog save your pa," he said.

"I can't find Shinglebolt!" Corky cried.

Cadje slid his arm around Corky's shoulders. He spoke softly. "Spirit dog gone. He spirit sent to help your pa. He come like that!" He snapped his fingers. "He gone like that!" He snapped them again. "He not real. Just spirit. *Good* spirit, though," he added.

Angrily, Corky shoved Cadje's arm away. "That's not true! Shinglebolt is *real*, and he's in trouble. We've got to find him and help him!" he cried.

Cadje lifted his peavey, moving toward the river. "Leave spirit alone. They come, they go. I not search for spirit. Bad medicine."

Desperately, Corky looked around for someone to help. All the shanty boys were working furiously, trying to keep the deluge of logs untangled. The swarming logs could form another jam.

Searching the river's surface, Corky moved downstream. Pa, missing his lucky green cap, waved at him from across the river. The rumbling of the logs blotted out his voice. Pa held his arms out, palms up, and shook his head mournfully. Corky understood what he meant. Pa thought Shinglebolt was dead, that he could not have survived. Pa motioned his arm across the river, pointed at Corky and shook his head. Corky understood that Pa wanted to cross the river to be with him, but there was no way to cross with the logs tumbling dangerously. Corky waved his understanding.

He trudged down river, scanning every foot of the river and both banks. Tears streamed down his cheeks. He kept squeezing his eyes together to clear his vision. *Oh, Shinglebolt! Where are you?* he sobbed, his shoulders shaking.

A hand touched his head, and Corky looked up, startled. It was Grandfather. The old man placed a gnarled finger below Corky's chin. "What's the matter, lad?" he asked.

Through jerking sobs, Corky told Grandfather what had happened, how Shinglebolt had saved Pa.

Grandfather's eyes flashed beneath his bushy brows. "Your father is safely past Snowtown Piers?"

Corky nodded, sniffling. "Because of Shinglebolt," he said. Corky's chin thrust out angrily. "Shinglebolt saved Pa, and now no one will help find Shinglebolt!"

Grandfather's face crinkled. "Of course we must find him, my boy. We shan't disregard his heroic deed. You and I will search until we find him, one way or the other."

Through tight jaws Corky mumbled, "You mean alive, or dead."

Grandfather touched Corky affectionately, his pale eyes looking deep into Corky's. "We shall hope to find him alive. But you must face the fact that it would be nearly a miracle for the great dog to survive such a tumult of rushing logs."

A new rush of tears poured from Corky's eyes.

Grandfather gave Corky a gentle shake. "Keep your hope up, my lad. Miracles happen every day. Why, the sun rising every morning is a kind of miracle." He squinted, scanning the river. "Now standing here sorrowing isn't doing our shaggy hero any good. We must examine every inch of the river and the shoreline. We must study the path of the current to discover where the flow would most likely carry him.

"Come." Grandfather climbed the embankment. "We shall stay as high as possible. This will give us a better view of the whole river bed."

Eyes aching from the concentration of staring at every portion of the river and its banks, Grandfather and Corky searched the river together. Lunch time passed, but neither thought of hunger.

Though hope continued to sink with every passing hour, Corky felt so grateful to Grandfather. He was trying hard to find Shinglebolt. He cared.

There were many false alarms. Globs of white foam from the agitated river looked amazingly like Shinglebolt's big white head. Again and again their hopes were lifted, then crushed. Once after Corky had scrambled eagerly down the bank to find only a whirl of foam swimming beside a log, he sighed, despairing. "Grandfather, Cadje says Shinglebolt was only a spirit, that he wasn't real. He thinks we'll never find him because he was just a ghost."

Grandfather grasped Corky's shoulders firmly. "No. Your heroic Shinglebolt was real. He may have been sent by a spiritual power to protect you and your father. I don't know. We shall never know. But he was real. And a finer dog never lived."

All afternoon they continued pacing the river. Grandfather pointed out swirls of current and eddies near shore which captured floating logs, debris, and perhaps, a huge St. Bernard. Their eyes searched the black logs and brown muddy river, seeking a spot of white or orange fur. Squinting and blinking, Corky concentrated, his heart thudding sadly in his chest. Time after time, when his eyes grew glassy, he shook his head to clear his vision.

Suddenly, with a shrill cackle, Grandfather pointed ahead. He gestured wildly toward a twisted pile of battered driftwood and hemlock boughs caught in the branches of an uprooted tree. Wide-eyed, Corky stared, but he saw no welcome white fur.

Grandfather hopped and bounced, shrieking, "The hat! The hat!"

Then Corky saw it, a splash of bright green caught in the tangled, floating debris. Pa's lucky cap!

In one jump Corky slid down the steep bank to the mass of driftwood and the green cap. As he reached out and clutched the cap, his arm brushed aside a broken hemlock bough. There before his startled eyes was Shinglebolt's big head. The dog's head and shoulders were caught in a fork of the overhanging branches.

With a scream Corky leaped into the shoulder-deep water. "It's him! It's him!" he shouted.

Grandfather slid into the cold water beside Corky. With a quick motion, he lifted Shinglebolt's closed eyelid and peered at the glazed eye beneath. Swiftly, he moved to the other side of the forked branch. "He's wedged in," he said. "We must lift him, then I'll push him toward you."

Grunting, they managed to free Shinglebolt's body and push him to shore, where the big head lay out of the water. Corky, panting and sobbing, began to shove Shinglebolt's hindquarters out of the water.

"No!" cried the old man. "Wait. We must handle him gently. He may be all broken up inside." Grandfather pulled off his deerskin jacket and motioned Corky to help him slide it under Shinglebolt's floating hindquarters. When the jacket was completely under the dog's shoulders and hindquarters, Grandfather said, "Now pull him up."

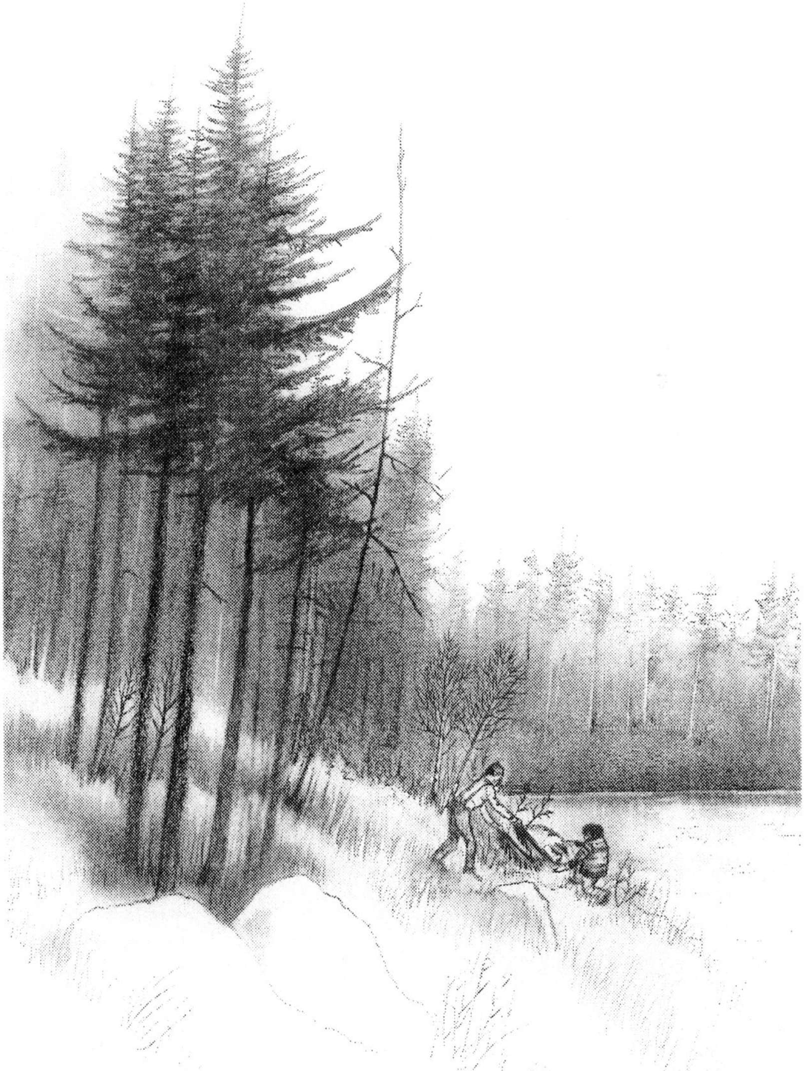

With the sodden deerskin jacket as a stretcher, they dragged the heavy dog out of the water.

Between sobs, Corky gasped, "Is he dead?"

Grandfather's hand pressed gently against Shinglebolt's rib cage. He wheezed, "His heart is beating, but faintly. Quickly, now, get some dry grass and leaves. We must warm him. He's been in cold water a long time."

Frantically, Corky gathered an armful of dry leaves and dumped them beside Shinglebolt. With both hands Grandfather gently rubbed dry grass against the soggy fur to absorb moisture.

"Get a fire going, lad," he ordered, as he continued blotting.

Corky's hands shook as he struggled with the kindling. His eyes kept flying to the still form of Shinglebolt. *He lies so still! Oh, Shinglebolt, why don't you move?*

As the fire crackled and began to give off warmth, Grandfather spoke. "Come here, boy. I want you to sit down beside Shinglebolt and stroke him, very gently. He's gone through a terrible battering. Speak to him softly. Call him by name. Talk right into his ear," he instructed.

Corky bent over the motionless body of his beloved friend, crooning softly, "Shinglebolt. I'm here now. I'm here, Shinglebolt. Oh, please, Shing, look at me. I love you so. Please don't die." He repeated the pleading litany for several minutes.

In despair, Corky looked up into his grandfather's wizened face. "He doesn't move."

Grandfather motioned impatiently. "Keep talking to him. Keep talking. You must call him back from the edge of death. You must make his spirit fight death. He loves you. Knowing you are with him may give him strength to come back."

Corky continued whispering and stroking the wet fur. Once the dog's muzzle twitched, and Corky's heart thumped hopefully. When there was no further movement, Corky's throat grew so tight he hardly could breathe. Soaked from his plunge into the river, Corky shivered, both from fear and cold, though the warmth of the fire spread around them.

A shudder rippled over the giant dog from shoulders to tail, and Corky gasped, alarmed. Then suddenly Shinglebolt's eyes opened. At first the glazed eyes stared blankly, then they grew clear. Very slowly the drenched white tail lifted and fell, lifted and fell again.

"Oh, Shing!" Corky cried, throwing his arms across Shinglebolt's shoulders.

"Careful, careful," cautioned Grandfather, easing Corky back.

Corky squirmed around to where he could look into Shinglebolt's soft brown eyes. He continued to stroke and croon to the dog, who lay perfectly still, except for his tail, which every few minutes thumped feebly.

As daylight began to fade, Shinglebolt's shallow breathing grew deeper and stronger. Dried by the warmth of the crackling fire, his fur began to fluff up. Corky's spirits rose. At last, with a grunt, Shinglebolt heaved himself sideways and rolled from lying on his side to an upright position.

Joyfully, Corky jumped to his feet. "Grandfather! He's going to be all right!"

Grandfather beamed. "I do believe so." Then, his sharp eyes piercing into Corky's, he added, "Another miracle has happened. You see, miracles happen all the time." He touched his grandson's cheek affectionately. "But sometimes we must help them along."

Corky threw himself into Grandfather's arms. "You're a miracle yourself, Grandfather. Without you, I'd never have found Shinglebolt. I'm so glad you're my grandfather."

A tear trickled down Grandfather's cheek. "I've been a long time without a family..." the wispy voice trailed off.

The bright campfire glowing on the dark river bank brought Cadje and Pa. Both men stopped, mouths gaping, when they caught sight of Shinglebolt resting in the circle of firelight. Shinglebolt turned doleful, drooping eyes on them. His tail, now dry and fluffy, thumped a welcome.

"I can't believe it!" Pa exclaimed, scratching his tousled head.

An impish twinkle in his eyes, Grandfather lifted the soggy green cap and thrust it toward Pa. "Your hat, Julius," he said ceremoniously. "Our heroic furry friend here not only saved *you*, but he managed to save your precious hat." His smiling face sobered as he added, "though he nearly lost his life doing so."

Pa clutched his lucky green-crowned cap and stared at it, shaking his head in amazement.

Cadje continued gaping at Shinglebolt. At last, he said quietly, "He *real*. Not spirit."

Grandfather smiled. "Of course he is a real dog, most assuredly of this world. But he is an uncommon creature, devoted and heroic.

How much better our world would be if we had more devotion and heroism such as his."

His dark eyes shining, Corky looked up at his father. "Grandfather helped me find Shinglebolt, Pa. I never would have found him without Grandfather." Corky clutched his grandfather's bony hand. "Grandfather must stay with us always and always." He looked pleadingly into Grandfather's face. "You *will* stay with us, won't you, *forever?*"

Grandfather and Pa gazed thoughtfully at each other across the campfire.

"The boy needs a teacher, Edward, if he is to stay with me," Pa said softly. "I'd be delighted if..."

Grandfather waved an arm impatiently. "Of course he needs a teacher. And he needs a grandfather, too. What do you think I'm here for?"

Pa chuckled. "I thought it had something to do with keeping me away from Snowtown Piers."

Grandfather snorted and rubbed his wiry beard. "That was the foolish raving of an old man too long separated from his loved ones. Snowtown Piers is but another dangerous bend in the river, no different from others."

Corky hugged his grandfather. "It's going to be wonderful, being together. All of us." He turned fondly toward the big St. Bernard. "You, too, Shinglebolt," he grinned.

With effort, Shinglebolt heaved himself to a standing position. Slowly and deliberately the great dog shook himself, sending a shower of sandy spray over Corky and the men. Corky threw his arms up, laughing joyfully.

His bushy white tail rotating wildly, Shinglebolt cocked his massive head. The furry corners of the dog's mouth pulled back, and his jowls wrinkled. Shinglebolt was smiling.

ORDER BLANK

Please send me the following books by Jean Cummings:
(indicate how many)

_____*Shinglebolt*	@ $10.95 each
_____*Buffalo in Our Backyard*	@$12.50 each
_____*Stardancer*	@ $12.50 each
_____*Alias the Buffalo Doctor*	@ $11.95 each

plus $3.00 shipping per book.
Michigan residents please add sales tax.

Mail to me at:

Name_____

Address_____

_____

If you would like your book or books autographed, please give instructions:

Please visit our Web site at:
http://members.aol.com/buffalodoctor/BDHOME.HTM

e-mail: BuffaloDoctor@aol.com

Mail your order to:
Jean Cummings
617 N. Tamiami Tr. #32
Venice, FL 34292

Bibliography

Allen, Clifford, State Supervisor, Harold Titus, <u>Michigan Log Marks</u>, Michigan State College, E. Lansing, 1941

Andrus, Percy H. "Historical Markers and Memorials in Michigan," <u>Michigan History Magazine</u>, Vol. XV, Spring No., 1931

"Annual of the Muskegon County Pioneer and Historical Society for the Year 1887" Hackley library

Ashley, Ray E. "Sawdust Days - The Rise and Fall of Lumber" typewritten copy Nov. 3, 1924, Hackley library

Bailey, John R. M.D. <u>Mackinac</u>, Robert Smith Printing Co., Lansing, Mich. 4th Edition, 1899 Hackley library

Bald, F. Clever, <u>Michigan in Four Centuries</u>, Harper & Brothers, N.Y. 1954 Big Rapids library

Beck, Earl Clifton, <u>Lore of the Lumber Camps</u>, University of Michigan Press, 1948, Ferris library

Beck, E. C. <u>They Knew Paul Bunyan</u>, Ann Arbor: The University of Michigan Press, 1956, Ferris Library

Beck, Earl Clifton, <u>Songs of the Michigan Lumberjacks</u>, University of Mich. Press, Ann Arbor, 1941 Hackley library

Beers, F. W. <u>County Atlas of Muskegon, Michigan</u>, Surveys of F. W. Beers, F. W. Beers & Co., N.Y. 1877

Burroughs, Raymond D. <u>Peninsular Country</u>, Wm. B. Eerdmans Pub. Co., Grand Rapids, 1965, Hackley library

Chapman Brothers, <u>Portrait and Biographical Album of Newaygo County, Mich</u>. Chicago, 1884

Conger, Louis H. "Indian and Trader Days at Muskegon" typewritten copy, The History Club, Sept. 1924, rearranged by author 1935 Hackley library

Cook, Samuel F. <u>Mackinaw in History</u>, Author's Edition Lansing, Mich. 1895 Hackley library

Craig, James Thomas "Muskegon and The Great Chicago Fire" typewritten 1944, Hackley library

Dunbar, Willis Frederick, Michigan Through the Centuries Vol. I, Lewis Historical Publishing Co., N.Y. 1955 Ferris library

Dunbar, Willis Frederick, Michigan: A History of the Wolverine State, Wm. B. Eerdmans Publishing Co., 1965

Fuller, George N. Ed. Historic Michigan, Vol I, and Vol. II, National Historical Assn. Inc. 1924 Big Rapids library

Fuller, George N. Economics and Social Beginnings of Michigan, Wynkoop Hollenbeck Crawford Co., Lansing, 1916

Glasgow, James, Muskegon, Michigan: The Evolution of a Lake Port The University of Chicago Libraries, Chicago, Ill. 1939 Hackley library

Goddard, Frederick B. Where to Emigrate and Why, The Peoples Publishing Co., Philadelphia, Penn. 1869

Graham, Samuel A. Aspens, University of Michigan Press Big Rapids Library

Hatcher, Harlan The Great Lakes, Oxford University Press N.Y. 1944 Big Rapids library

Hatcher, Harlan and Erich A. Walter, A Pictorial History of the Great Lakes, Bonanza Books, N.Y. 1963

Havighurst, Walter, Three Flags at the Straits, The Forts of Mackinac, Prentice-Hall Inc. 1966

Hinsdale, W. B. The First People of Michigan, George Wahr, Ann Arbor, 1930, Hackley library

Hinsdale, W. B. Primitive Man in Michigan, Michigan Handbook Series No. 1, University of Michigan Press, 1925, Hackley library

Holbrook, Stewart H. Holy Old Mackinaw, subtitled "Natural History of the American Lumberjack," New York, 1928. Big Rapids library

Holbrook, Stewart H., Tall Timber, The MacMillan Co., N.Y. 1041, Big Rapids library

Holbrook, Stewart Burning an Empire

Holt, Henry H "Centennial History of Muskegon" carbon copy of typewritten manuscript 23 ppgs. Hackley library

Hubbard, Gurdon Saltonstall, The Autobiography of Gurdon Saltonstall Hubbard, Pa-Pa-Ma-Ti-Pe "The Swift Walker," The Lakeside Press, Chicago, R. R. Donnelly and Sons Co.,, 1911

Johnson, The Michigan Fur Trade, Michigan Historical Commission, Lansing, 1919 Ferris library

Kelton, Dwight H. Annals of Fort Mackinac, Jacker Edition, 1891 Hackley library

Kincitz, W. Vernon, The Indians of the Western Great Lakes 1615-1760; University of Michigan Press, Ann Arbor, 1940

Kyes, Alice Prescott The Romance of Muskegon, Michigan 1937 Centennial Year by Muskegon Chronicle, published by Muskegon Public Schools, 1971 Hackley library

Lewis, Ferris E. Michigan Yesterday and Today, Hillsdale School Supply, Hillsdale, Mich. 1956 Big Rapids library

Lewis, Ferris E. Handbook for the Teaching of Michigan History, Hillsdale School Supply, Inc. Hillsdale, Mich. 1964 Ferris library

May, George S. Pictorial History of Michigan, Wm. B. Eerdmans Publishing Co., Grand Rapids, 1967

Maybee, Rolland H. Michigan's White Pine Era 1840-1900

Mecosta County Album, Chicago, 1883

Michigan Pioneer Collections, Volumes XXX and XXI

Morley, Michigan centennial booklet

Lewis, Ferris E. Michigan Yesterday and Today, Hillsdale School Supply, Hillsdale, Mich. 1956 Big Rapids library

Michigan Historical Commission, Lansing, 1960 Hackley library

McKee, Russell, Great Lakes Country, Thomas Y. Crowell Co., N.Y. 1966, Big Rapids library

Michigan State Administrative Board, Michigan, A Guide to the Wolverine State, Oxford University Press, N.Y. 1941

Page & Co., H.R. History of Muskegon County, Michigan, 1882

Patterson, Lillie Lumberjacks of the North Woods, Garrard Publishing Co. Champaign, Ill. 1967

Quaife, Milo M. <u>Lake Michigan</u>, The American Lakes Series, The Bobbs Merrill Co, 1944, Big Rapids library

Quimby, <u>Indian Life in the Upper Great Lakes</u>

Repplier, Agnes, <u>Pere Marquette, Priest, Pioneer and Adventurer</u>, Doubleday, Doran and Co., Inc. Garden City, N.Y. 1929 Hackley library

Schoolcraft, Henry R. <u>Narrative Journal of Travels, in the year 1820</u>, edited by Mentor L. Williams, Michigan State College Press, 1953, Hackley library

Scott, I. D. <u>Inland Lakes of Michigan</u>, Wynkoop Hollenbeck Crawford Co., Lansing, Mich. 1921

Spooner, Harry L. "The First White Pathfinders of Newaygo County, Michigan" (unpublished manuscript) Ferris library

Tacksbury, <u>Atlas of State of Michigan,</u> Detroit, Mich. 1873

Waitley, Douglas, <u>Portrait of the Midwest</u>, Abelard-Schuman, N.Y.1963

Williams, Meade C. <u>Early Mackinac</u>, Duffield & Co., N.Y. 1912, Hackley library

Hubbard, Gurdon Saltonstall, The Autobiography of Gurdon Saltonstall Hubbard, Pa-Pa-Ma-Ti-Pe "The Swift Walker," The Lakeside Press, Chicago, R. R. Donnelly and Sons Co.,, 1911

Johnson, The Michigan Fur Trade, Michigan Historical Commission, Lansing, 1919 Ferris library

Kelton, Dwight H. Annals of Fort Mackinac, Jacker Edition, 1891 Hackley library

Kincitz, W. Vernon, The Indians of the Western Great Lakes 1615-1760; University of Michigan Press, Ann Arbor, 1940

Kyes, Alice Prescott The Romance of Muskegon, Michigan 1937 Centennial Year by Muskegon Chronicle, published by Muskegon Public Schools, 1971 Hackley library

Lewis, Ferris E. Michigan Yesterday and Today, Hillsdale School Supply, Hillsdale, Mich. 1956 Big Rapids library

Lewis, Ferris E. Handbook for the Teaching of Michigan History, Hillsdale School Supply, Inc. Hillsdale, Mich. 1964 Ferris library

May, George S. Pictorial History of Michigan, Wm. B. Eerdmans Publishing Co., Grand Rapids, 1967

Maybee, Rolland H. Michigan's White Pine Era 1840-1900

Mecosta County Album, Chicago, 1883

Michigan Pioneer Collections, Volumes XXX and XXI

Morley, Michigan centennial booklet

Lewis, Ferris E. Michigan Yesterday and Today, Hillsdale School Supply, Hillsdale, Mich. 1956 Big Rapids library

Michigan Historical Commission, Lansing, 1960 Hackley library

McKee, Russell, Great Lakes Country, Thomas Y. Crowell Co., N.Y. 1966, Big Rapids library

Michigan State Administrative Board, Michigan, A Guide to the Wolverine State, Oxford University Press, N.Y. 1941

Page & Co., H.R. History of Muskegon County, Michigan, 1882

Patterson, Lillie Lumberjacks of the North Woods, Garrard Publishing Co. Champaign, Ill. 1967

Quaife, Milo M. <u>Lake Michigan</u>, The American Lakes Series, The Bobbs Merrill Co, 1944, Big Rapids library

Quimby, <u>Indian Life in the Upper Great Lakes</u>

Repplier, Agnes, <u>Pere Marquette, Priest, Pioneer and Adventurer</u>, Doubleday, Doran and Co., Inc. Garden City, N.Y. 1929 Hackley library

Schoolcraft, Henry R. <u>Narrative Journal of Travels, in the year 1820</u>, edited by Mentor L. Williams, Michigan State College Press, 1953, Hackley library

Scott, I. D. <u>Inland Lakes of Michigan</u>, Wynkoop Hollenbeck Crawford Co., Lansing, Mich. 1921

Spooner, Harry L. "The First White Pathfinders of Newaygo County, Michigan" (unpublished manuscript) Ferris library

Tacksbury, <u>Atlas of State of Michigan,</u> Detroit, Mich. 1873

Waitley, Douglas, <u>Portrait of the Midwest</u>, Abelard-Schuman, N.Y.1963

Williams, Meade C. <u>Early Mackinac</u>, Duffield & Co., N.Y. 1912, Hackley library